Door
ᵒᶠ *Hope*

LINCOLN SQUARE SERIES
BOOK 2

Anna Huckabee

Relax. Read. Repeat.

DOOR OF HOPE (Lincoln Square Series, Book 2)
By Anna Huckabee
Published by TouchPoint Press
Brookland, AR 72417
www.touchpointpress.com

ISBN 13: 978-1-946920-53-9
ISBN 10: 1-946920-53-3

Editor: Melody Millier
Cover Design: RedWritingHoodInk.net

http://AnnaHuckabee.com/

If you are new to the Lincoln Square series, be sure to grab *Talents* (Book 1) today!

First Edition

Printed in the United States of America

To my grandmas: Anna Spilger and Mildred Brush. You taught me to always look for the good in people. You taught me to love even when it was difficult to do so. You taught me to quilt. I want to be like you when I grow up. I love you!

From there, I will give her vineyards to her,
and the Valley of Achor as a door of hope.
She will respond there as in the days of her youth,
and as in the day when she came up out of the land of Egypt.
—Prophet Hosea

Chapter One

Early morning sunlight streamed in through the bedroom window. The smell of coffee with a hint of bacon drifted into the room. A whisk clattered against a mixing bowl, followed by the metallic thunk of a griddle against the stove.

Carly groaned. She lay in bed, awake, wishing she could close her eyes and disappear.

Her eyes traveled around her bedroom—the same one she'd had since childhood. Sure, it had been redecorated a time or two since she was in grade school. The fading pictures and frilly curtains mocked Carly, a reminder that life had not gone the way she'd planned when she was eighteen.

This morning, of all mornings, was worse than most.

Carly rolled toward the wall with another groan. She wished she could pull a blanket of darkness around herself and escape from this day. A tear slid down her cheek.

Footsteps echoed up the hall outside Carly's room. Her door opened without a knock. Her mom peeked through the opening.

"Happy birthday!"

Carly groaned again and didn't move.

"You are usually up by now. I made your favorite—waffles and bacon."

Carly rolled over and sat up. Even on her birthday, she wasn't allowed to sleep late. Not that she could if she tried. All she wanted was to lay there and be miserable.

"I liked waffles when I was twelve, Mom." She pushed the sheet back and swung her legs over the edge of the bed.

Her mom's face fell. "I'm sorry. I thought I could do something special. Cereal didn't seem like a very good birthday breakfast."

Carly felt a twinge of guilt. "No. It's okay. Thanks for making them." She tried to smile. Sliding her feet into her slippers, she shuffled across the room to her desk. "I'll be right there. Give me a minute."

Carly opened her laptop and checked her email. Nothing. Not one response to any of the dozens of job applications she'd sent out in the last few weeks. She checked the job websites for any new postings. Nothing there, either.

Happy birthday to me, thought Carly. She covered her face with her hands. She'd been laid off from her job weeks ago and had to move back home. Worst of all, her mom still treated her like she was a child.

Carly pushed away from the desk and shuffled up the hall to the kitchen for breakfast.

Her dad sat at the table sipping coffee and reading the news. He looked up and smiled his good morning, then went back to his reading. Carly sat down.

"Happy birthday," he said, without looking up.

Carly looked at her dad. He was smiling. He glanced up at her again. His eyes twinkled.

"Got you a little something." He pushed a tiny box across the table toward her.

Carly picked it up, untied the ribbon on the top, and opened the lid. She pulled out the jewelry box inside and opened it. A necklace with a dove pendant rested on the velvet pillow. The dove had her birthstone in the middle.

"The stone is real," her dad said, a measure of pride in his voice. He grinned at her with childish delight, then looked back at his paper.

Carly pulled the necklace out of the box and let the pendant lay in her palm. "I'll never take it off," she said. "I love it!"

"Don't know why we never got you jewelry before," Dad shrugged. "I guess we didn't think about it. You always ask for more practical things."

Mom walked into the room with a plate of waffles and set it on the table in front of Carly. Her eyes widened when she saw her dad's gift now hanging around Carly's neck.

"Oh! You gave her the necklace! It looks lovely! Happy birthday, honey."

Carly smiled at her mom and took a waffle. She wasn't a breakfast person. She felt sick to her stomach at the thought of eating. But not wanting to hurt her mom's feelings, she drizzled syrup on it and jabbed it with her fork.

"Any news about a job?" Dad asked as he set his paper aside to eat breakfast.

"Not this morning. I'll have to check the job classifieds in the paper. Three weeks and still nothing."

"I invited Dale, Jessie, and the kids for supper tonight so we could all celebrate your birthday as a family. They haven't been over in a while. I thought it would be nice," Mom said between sips of coffee, unaware of the conversation that had been taking place around her. "You'll get the rest of your presents then."

Both Carly and her dad looked up at her, then at each other. The corner of Dad's lip twitched, and he ducked his head to look at his food once more. Carly rolled her eyes.

"I wish you wouldn't have, Mom." Carly couldn't keep the rebuke out of her voice. "I don't feel like it. I'd rather spend the evening with you and Dad."

"You need to be around people more. Besides, it's just your brother and his family. It'll be good for you." Mom picked up the carafe and carried it back to the kitchen for more coffee.

Carly looked to her dad for help. "Please. Dad. Can you talk her out of this? I don't want to be around people today."

"I think it's too late for that. She started preparing the food yesterday, and she ordered a cake. Don't tell her I told! She wants to help you, Carly. I'd be down, too. Let her help." Dad reached out and gave her hand a squeeze.

"It isn't helping," Carly muttered. She couldn't bring herself to put another bite in her mouth. Swallowing the last of her coffee, she stood up, grabbed the classifieds, and planted a kiss on her dad's cheek.

"I'm going to my room to look for a job. Thanks for the necklace, Dad. I really do love it."

Carly turned, left the breakfast table, and shut herself in her room before her mom returned.

Chapter Two

Carly huddled in the corner of the couch. On the other side of the room, Dad and Dale discussed business models and whether or not the economy could support new start-ups. Mom and Jessie cleaned the kitchen. Carly had offered to help, but they'd shooed her out. She could hear them talking, Jessie sharing the children's latest antics and Mom laughing about them. The kids were in Dale's old room, laughing and screaming while they played.

Carly rubbed her temple with the tips of her fingers and let herself retreat into her thoughts. Misery swirled in her mind, darkening her mood. Last year, she'd spent her birthday with friends from work. They'd gone out for supper, then caught a movie. She hadn't gotten back to her apartment until late. She'd celebrated with her parents the next Saturday. It had been small, quiet, just the three of them.

She hadn't heard from those "friends" in over a month. For the first week or two after she'd been laid off, they'd texted now and then. Once, one of them asked her to meet them for a meal after work. Carly didn't have the money. She told them she might be able to come another time. They hadn't texted since then. So much for friends.

This year was neither small nor quiet. Nothing like the birthday party she had in mind. But then, they never bothered to ask what she wanted.

A headache throbbed behind Carly's eyes. She squeezed them shut and rubbed her temple harder to see if it would go away. If only the kids would stop screaming.

Carly considered slipping out of the living room and going to her bedroom for the rest of the evening. Would anyone even notice if she disappeared?

The phone rang. The sound jerked Carly away from her dark thoughts. She heard her mom answer it in the kitchen. A moment later Mom entered the living room, face pale.

"That…that was Walter. Mom…" Her voice caught. She cleared her throat and fought to continue. "Mom collapsed tonight. They've taken her to St. Mary's. I need to go."

Dad leaped out of his chair. "I'm coming with you."

Mom nodded and turned around, searching for what to do next. Carly jumped to her feet. She found her mom's purse and a light jacket in the closet and pressed the things into her mom's hands.

"Sometimes it's cold in hospitals."

"Yes. Yes, of course." Mom murmured, dazed.

Dad took Mom's arm and led her toward the front door. His eyes met Carly's across the room. They held more apology than his words.

"I'm sorry," he said.

Carly managed a smile. "It's okay, Dad. I was hoping for a quiet evening at home. I'm sure Grandma will be okay."

Carly turned to look at Dale and Jessie. The three of them stood in stunned silence in the living room. The noise from the children's play died down as one by one the children trickled into the living room.

"What happened, Dad?" Mark, the oldest, was the first to break the silence.

"I don't know, Great-grandma fell and had to go to the hospital. Grandma and Grandpa went to be with her and Uncle Walter."

"Is she going to die?" Olivia, the youngest, asked.

"I don't know yet, sweetheart," Dale said. "We need to pray for her, and for Grandma and Uncle Walter."

"Because they're her kids and they don't want her to die," Olivia stated.

"Yes. Look," Dale turned to Carly. "We don't have to hang around. I have to get to work early tomorrow, and the kids need to get to bed."

"We didn't have cake," Jessie said. "It's an ice cream cake. Susan set it out so it would soften. Why don't we have it before we go? We can sing and have candles."

"No singing," Carly was emphatic.

"Ah, come on," Jessie said. "For the kids?"

"No. Not for the kids. Not for me. Not for any reason at all."

Dale chuckled. "Drop it, Jess. We're cut from the same cloth. The cake will taste just as good without any singing."

The family trooped into the kitchen. The cake was cut and eaten in silence. Carly and Jessie loaded the last of the dishes into the dishwasher, while Dale got the kids busy cleaning up their mess.

Then they piled into their car and left, taking all the noise and activity with them.

Carly stood in the quiet living room alone. She tried watching television, then reading a book, but she couldn't concentrate. She retired to her bedroom to try reading in bed instead of on the couch.

A quilt lay over the bed, a quilt Grandma had made for Carly when she turned twenty-one. They'd shopped for the fabric together. Grandma had helped her cut it out and piece it; then she'd quilted it during Carly's last year at college. It didn't match the rest of her bedroom. The deep teal, green, and blue reminded Carly of the ocean. She'd saved the quilt for years in a hope chest until it became apparent to her that she wasn't going to be needing it for her own home.

Carly walked to the bed and pulled the quilt back. She wrapped herself in its folds and thought about her grandma lying in a hospital bed, her future uncertain. Grandma, who'd always understood her. Who'd listened to her talk about her dreams and plans and comforted her through disappointments. Who'd always let her be her own person. Who loved Carly just the way she was.

The sobs came. They wracked Carly's body. She cried until she started hiccoughing and then cried some more. She'd lost so much the last few weeks. She couldn't lose Grandma, too.

Carly cried herself to sleep.

***

Carly woke sometime in the night when the front door opened and closed. She heard her parents talking. Footsteps came up the hall, then her door opened. Mom stuck her head inside.

"Are you still awake? I saw your light on."

Carly muttered something, still groggy. She pushed the covers back and leaned on her elbow. "How's Grandma?"

"She's improving. They are going to do more tests tomorrow to see if they can find out what happened."

Another sob caught in Carly's throat. "Thank God!"

"Sorry your birthday was ruined. We'll have to make it up to you another time, maybe when Grandma is out of the hospital."

"It's okay, Mom. My birthday was fine. You look beat. Go to bed. Hopefully, we'll have good news in the morning."

Mom gave Carly a strained smile and shut the door behind her.

Carly reached over and turned off her lamp. She wrapped herself in the quilt again, and sleep claimed her once more.

Chapter Three

"They can't find anything wrong with her," Uncle Walter said. He looked down at his cup of coffee. "They've ruled out all the big things—stroke, heart attack, seizures, tumors, cancer. He said he thinks Mom is getting old."

The whole family sat in the cafeteria at the hospital while Uncle Walter shared the doctor's report.

"He says she can go home tomorrow if—and he said it was a huge if—she has someone staying with her at all times." Uncle Walter looked around the room at the family. "I've been checking into live-in care, and it will be quite expensive. I don't know if Mom can afford it. I don't even think the rest of us could if we pooled our resources."

He hesitated. "That brings me to an option that Ellen thought of just before you all arrived."

Walter turned to Carly. "I know you lost your job a few weeks ago. I also know how well you and Mom get on. Would you think about moving in with Mom so she can live at home? We can have a nurse come in several days a week to check on her. You'd have to be there with her in case of emergencies."

Surprised, Carly stared at her uncle. She hesitated only for a moment. "Yes. I don't even need time to think about it. I'd love to stay with Grandma."

"Good. Well, then, I'll go tell Ellen and the doctor, and we can start getting Mom released."

"You sure you want to do this?" Dad asked as they rode home together later that morning.

"Positive." Carly felt more and more confident in her decision. "It's a way I can help Grandma. And I can't seem to find any other job. Maybe I'm meant to do this."

"This is the most upbeat I've seen you in a while," Dad remarked. He glanced at Carly out of the corner of his eye. "Your mom and I are worried about you, you know."

Carly glanced out the car window. She thought for a while before she answered.

"I don't know what the trouble is. I feel like my life is a series of dead-end streets. I feel like I haven't been able to live my life the way I'd always planned."

Her dad nodded. "There's nothing wrong with being disappointed over lost dreams and hopes. That's normal. You need to move on and make new plans and dreams that will replace those you lost."

"I don't know if I can." Carly looked out the window. "What if I lose those, too?"

"I don't know what to tell you there, sweetheart. You are an amazing, intelligent woman. I hate to see you pining for things that will never be and missing out on all the wonderful things you could be doing."

Carly shook her head. "I have no wonderful things that I should be doing. Life is moving forward for everyone but me." She fell silent. A tear slid unchecked down her cheek.

"Life is moving forward for you, too. You have to choose to live it." Her dad joined her in silence until they pulled into the driveway at home. "I'll get a suitcase for you."

***

Carly felt a twinge of horror as she walked through Grandma's house that afternoon. A fine film of dust covered everything. Cobwebs hung from the ceiling and drifted across the multitude of photographs that covered the walls. When Carly opened the drapes to let in the afternoon sunlight, billows of dust came out. It thickened the layer on all the furniture and sent Carly into a coughing fit.

The trash cans were full to overflowing. The kitchen counter was piled with dirty dishes. Carly could see places where Grandma had tried to clear things up but hadn't had the strength to continue.

She walked through the house to the guest room. Aside from needing a good dusting, it was clean. The bathroom was another story.

"I've been out of work. I could have helped her with this," Carly muttered to herself as she surveyed the room.

Carly put her things in the guest room. Then she cleaned the bathroom while her mom cleaned the kitchen. They both worked in Grandma's room and the living room. A couple of hours later the rooms were at least livable.

Her mom was reluctant to leave. She puttered around for a long time, finding little things to do here and there.

"Mom, you can go. I'll be fine by myself." Carly tried not to sound impatient or irritated.

"Are you sure? I hate to leave you here alone."

"Some of us don't mind being alone, Mom."

"You sound like your father. Okay, I'll go. But if you need anything, don't hesitate to call. We'll be here as quick as we can. I'm not sure about this neighborhood."

"I'll be fine, Mom," Carly repeated. She wanted to add, "I'm a grown woman. I don't need your help with this anymore," but she stopped herself.

"Right. Okay. Uncle Walter will bring Mom in the morning as soon as they release her. He'll have a better idea of when the nurses will be coming and what all your responsibilities will be. Be careful!"

Carly closed the door behind her mom. She turned back to Grandma's living room and looked around. Then she walked to the couch, sank into its cushions, and basked in the silence that surrounded her.

Chapter Four

Uncle Walter and Grandma arrived the following morning. Grandma made her way into the house with help from both Uncle Walter and Carly. She sank into her easy chair in the living room with a deep sigh.

Carly hadn't slept well in the guest room bed, and she'd been up early cleaning. The quiet of the house along with the work should have been cathartic. Instead, misery washed over her in waves and that deep, gut-wrenching feeling that her life was a failure threatened to overwhelm her. Grandma's arrival was a relief.

Uncle Walter took Carly aside. He showed her a schedule of medications Grandma needed. Another page had a schedule of when the in-home nurse would be visiting and their responsibilities. Carly posted the lists on the refrigerator. He gave her some money to use for food and anything else they might need. Then he checked the mail and took out the bills.

"Why don't you stay for lunch?" Carly said.

"Not today. I'm going to get a half day in at the office. Your mom was at the hospital. She said she was going to try to come over this afternoon to see if you need anything."

Carly rolled her eyes. "Seriously. I don't know what she's worried about. I've got this."

Uncle Walter chuckled. "I suspect she's more worried about Mom than you. She is also feeling guilty for being so busy the last few weeks. You're going to have to tolerate your Mom being clingy for a while."

Mom is always clingy, thought Carly.

After Uncle Walter left, she added the final touches to the soup she'd made and got the crackers from the pantry. Despite the hot summer weather, the soup sounded good.

Carly walked back into the living room. Grandma had her feet up and her eyes closed. She opened them when she heard Carly.

"When do you want lunch, Grandma?"

"Let me rest my eyes for a little while. I don't want to keep you, but I'm tired. I didn't sleep well at all the last few nights."

"I imagine not," Carly said. "I don't see how anyone can sleep in a hospital with all the lights and noise and people coming in and out at all hours. It's soup. I'll turn it off and heat it again when you've rested."

"Thank you so much, you dear girl. I'm glad you're going to be here to keep me company. An old woman gets lonely puttering around in a house all by herself." Grandma smiled up at Carly.

Carly gently squeezed the old lady's hand and left the room. She could finish cleaning her room while she waited.

An hour passed, then two hours. Grandma slept in the chair. Carly finished cleaning the guest room—her room now. Then she moved to the kitchen pantry. She cleaned, straightened, and dusted. She threw items away that were out of date and rearranged it so she could find things when she wanted them.

Carly looked at the list of medications. Grandma was supposed to have taken two of the pills already. One of them couldn't be taken with another pill that was due in only thirty minutes. She couldn't decide if she should wake Grandma or not. The phone rang.

Grandma stirred and Carly hurried to answer it.

"Hi, sweetie," her mom said on the other end. "I'm on my way over. Do you need me to bring anything?"

"Not right now, Mom."

Carly poked her head around the corner into the living room. Grandma sat up in the chair and put her feet down.

Carly went back into the living room as Grandma stood. "Do you need help?" she asked. Grandma had always been able to take care of herself. Now she looked thin and frail.

The old woman shuffled toward her, legs stiff from sitting too long. "I'll be fine for now. Just need to use the little girl's room."

"Lunch is ready, and you have some pills you need to take."

Grandma gripped the wall for support as she went up the hall. "I can smell the food. It smells so much better than hospital food."

Carly turned on the stove to reheat the soup. She set out bowls and spoons. Then she put Grandma's pills in a small cup next to her bowl. She fidgeted while she waited.

Grandma came into the kitchen about the time the soup was hot enough to eat. She sank into her usual seat and reached for the pills.

"Amazing how normal activities can tucker out an old woman." She sighed as she reached for her glass of water. "I'm not as spry as I used to be."

Carly set the soup on the table and ladled some into the bowls. She kissed Grandma's cheek. Then she sat down in the other kitchen chair. "You'll get it back. None of us knew how sick you were."

"I didn't know how sick I was, or I would have said something. I'm thankful your Aunt Ellen found me when she did." Grandma's hand shook as she brought the first bite of soup to her mouth.

Carly's mom arrived while they ate. She fussed over Grandma while Carly cleaned up the kitchen.

"Your Grandma says you might need some groceries. Do you want to go through things and make a list?" Mom asked when Carly joined the other two women.

Carly flinched at the condescension in her mother's voice. "I looked through the pantry and fridge this morning. We should be fine for a few days, maybe a week." Carly tried to keep her voice calm.

"Well, call if you need something." Susan smiled at Carly, then patted Grandma on the arm. "I'm thankful you are doing better."

Carly left the room. She couldn't handle her mother's condescension. She closed herself in her room and read until she heard her mom leave.

Chapter Five

Carly didn't sleep well again that night. Every sound, every creak of the floorboards, woke her. Grandma coughed and Carly dove out of bed and flew to her room, but that was the only sound she made. The older woman slept soundly, her even breathing broken by the occasional snore.

She sought the coffee pot in the morning. The carafe contained several dead roaches and a spider. Carly gagged hard several times as she dumped them into the trash. She tried not to throw the carafe into the sink.

To distract herself, she went in search of coffee grounds. After looking through the pantry and refrigerator, she found a tiny bag in the back of the freezer with enough left for one pot of coffee, two if she made them weak.

Carly sank into a kitchen chair and swiped a tear away with her palm. All she wanted was some coffee. A good night's sleep wouldn't hurt, either. She looked up at the side of the refrigerator. A little notepad and pen hung there. Carly stood and took the pen and paper and began her grocery list.

The coffee was almost done brewing when Grandma walked into the little kitchen.

"Did you sleep well, dear?"

Carly sighed. "No. I have to get used to the new house sounds and the new bed."

"I should give you one of my sleeping pills," Grandma commented. "I take one, and I'm out for the whole night."

Grandma was taking sleeping pills? Carly scowled at her back.

"Coffee!" Grandma exclaimed. "I haven't had a good cup of coffee in a long time. No sense in getting out the pot when I'm here alone."

Carly set out two mugs, dusted them, and checked for nasty bugs. "I'm not sure it's a good cup of coffee. I found the grounds in the back of the freezer. We'll have to get some more when we do our shopping."

Grandma grinned like a little kid with candy. "It's better than what they had at the hospital."

After breakfast had been cleared and the few dishes washed, Carly helped Grandma get settled in her chair. Grandma turned on a morning talk show. The visiting nurse wouldn't arrive for another hour.

Carly returned to the kitchen. She knew she ought to take everything out of the cupboards and clean them. Uncle Walter or Dad would need to come in and spray for bugs.

Carly stood and stared at the open cabinets, imagining the horrors they contained. An involuntary shudder shook her body. She couldn't do it. Not this morning. She turned and left the kitchen, slipped down the hall to her room, and picked up a book.

***

Carly jerked awake. She looked at the clock. She'd been asleep for over an hour. The sound of a man's voice floated down the hall. She rubbed the sleep out of her eyes. Who could be here?

Carly pushed herself up to sit on the edge of the bed and struggled to remember what she was supposed to be doing instead of napping.

Grandma! The visiting nurse! Carly jumped to her feet and hurried out of the room and down the hall. She stopped when she reached the living room.

The nurse knelt on the floor next to Grandma's chair. He pressed his stethoscope to Grandma's elbow as he watched the dial. He didn't look up until he finished. Then he smiled up at Grandma and began removing the cuff.

"Your blood pressure looks good, Mrs. Terrell, as does your blood sugar. I need to check your legs for swelling, and then we can get you up for a walk." He stopped speaking, rose to his feet, and looked at Carly.

The nurse was very tall—well over six feet—and fit. He was probably the best-looking man Carly had ever seen, despite a long scar that went up his neck onto his chin and the lower part of his cheek. He was not wearing a wedding ring. Carly felt guilty for noticing. For even checking. She felt her face grow hot.

"Hi, I'm Will. I'm the nurse assigned to your Grandma. I'll be in three days a week. There might be other nurses occasionally, but they like to keep us on the same cases so we can pick up on potential problems."

Carly nodded. Will hadn't seemed to notice her red face. "It's nice to meet you. I'm Carly."

"I'm pretty much done in here. Her doctor wants her to get up and take a walk every day. We're going to see how far she makes it up the street today." He turned to Grandma with a grin. "Ready?"

Carly watched them as they left. Grandma chatted with Will as they shuffled along. He laughed at some story she told. Then she laughed back. She tired before they reached the next driveway and he turned them around for her to come back.

Carly disappeared into the kitchen before they got back. She didn't want to see Will again. She started pulling things out of the refrigerator for lunch.

"I'm going now, but I'll be back on Thursday."

Carly almost jumped out of her skin at the sound of Will's voice behind her. She jerked around.

"Don't sneak up on a person like that!"

He laughed. "Sorry! I wanted to ask if you would be able to get your Grandma out for a walk tomorrow. She needs to walk as far as she can every day."

"Sure," Carly said. "I need to go to the grocery store. She can come with me, and I'll get her to walk as far as she can and then push her in a wheelchair the rest of the time."

"That's good. She needs to get out around other people and have a change of scenery now and then."

He turned back to the living room. "Bye, Mrs. Terrell. See you in a couple of days. I'll let myself out."

Once he was gone, Carly carried a glass of water to Grandma. She leaned back in her chair with her feet up as high as the footrest would go. Her eyes were closed. Carly thought she might be sleeping, but she opened her eyes when Carly approached.

"Oh, thank you.". Grandma sat up and reached for the glass. "It's hot out there today."

Carly walked around to the other easy chair and sank into it.

"You've been quiet lately. I remember when you were a child we almost couldn't get you to stop talking." Grandma chuckled at the memory.

Carly smiled at her. It annoyed her when her mom said things like that. When Grandma said it, Carly knew she was just sharing a memory.

"I don't feel like talking, Grandma. I don't always know what to say." Carly sighed. "I thought maybe you would need a little extra peace and quiet for a couple of days. It's like going on vacation and then coming home. You have to rest up from all that resting."

Grandma laughed again. "I'd argue that being in the hospital is hardly a vacation."

Carly choked up and tears clouded her eyes as she thought about how close she'd come to losing her grandma. She came across the room and squeezed the old lady's hand. She muttered something about making sure the lunch didn't burn and hurried to the kitchen. A tear slid down her cheek despite all her efforts to stop it.

Chapter Six

The heat hung on for the rest of the week. Grandma couldn't handle walking outside for long, and she was exhausted afterward.

Friday was her first doctor's appointment after her release from the hospital. Carly took her to the appointment and parked in the handicapped space closest to the door. The distance from the car to the door looked a football field away.

"Are you up for this, Grandma?" Carly turned off the car and unbuckled her seatbelt. "I can drive around and drop you off at the door."

"No, the doctor says I need the exercise." Grandma didn't sound convinced.

"I'm not sure even he would think it wise in this heat. I can walk you from the door to the elevator inside."

"Then I'd be all out of breath when I got up to his office. No, I'll get it over with now. Besides, I read an article once that said that people are more likely to stick with exercise if they do it outside." Grandma fumbled with her belt and opened the car door. "Let's get this over with."

"I'm not sure this is what the article meant," Carly muttered to herself as she hurried around the car.

She gripped Grandma's arm as the elderly lady shoved herself out of the seat. With confident steps, Grandma walked across the drive and onto the sidewalk where an orderly met them with a wheelchair. Carly whispered her thanks to him and helped Grandma into the chair. Carly pushed her the rest of the way inside the hospital.

The cool air of the lobby hit them as the doors opened with a soft "whoosh." Carly pulled out a bottle of water. "Here, drink this Grandma. It'll help."

Grandma took a few grateful swallows and then handed the bottle back. Her hands were shaking. She closed her eyes. They rested in the lobby for a few minutes before taking the elevator to the appointment.

After the nurse took Grandma back to see the doctor, Carly tried to read a magazine she found on a side table. The television blared a soap opera. The noise of a radio playing music drifted from behind the receptionist's window. Carly gave up. She leaned her head against the wall and closed her eyes.

"Miss Warren?" The nurse's voice calling her name jerked Carly out of her reverie. "The doctor would like you to come back for a few minutes."

Carly stood and followed the woman back to a small examining room. Grandma was still in the wheelchair. The doctor sat on a rolling stool in front of her. He motioned for Carly to sit on the examination table.

"I understand you are caring for Mrs. Terrell in an ongoing capacity?"

"Yes," Carly answered.

"She claims to feel fine, although a little tired. Is there anything you've noticed that would give cause for concern?"

"No. She is eating well, sleeping at night, and getting out for daily exercise."

He nodded and made some notes on the chart. "Good. I want you to watch for these symptoms: disorientation or confusion, dizziness, extreme fatigue, inability to move a limb or swallow, inability to focus her eyes, headaches, swelling in the extremities, tightness in her chest or shortness of breath. I'll send a paper home with you."

Carly nodded, thinking of the growing number of papers posted on the refrigerator.

"Any of those things, no matter how minor, are reason to call my office. I'll want to see her, and she should be brought to the hospital," he continued. "Also, she should avoid people with known communicable diseases, even the common cold."

Grandma cleared her throat and glared at the doctor. "Am I to be housebound, then?"

The doctor looked up at her as if he'd forgotten she was there. "No, I don't think so. But your family and friends should stay away if they are sick."

"What about the heat?" Carly asked. "It takes a lot out of her to be out walking around in it."

"Maybe you could go to the store or the mall, and she can walk as much as is comfortable for her. But outdoor exercise is best. She needs the sunlight. Okay, I think that's everything. I'll see you again in a month." The doctor stood and left the room.

Carly slid off the table and collected Grandma's purse from the small desk in the corner. Then she unlocked the wheels of the chair and pushed her toward the door just as a nurse opened it.

"I came to see if you needed help," she said. She held the door while Carly pushed her grandma out of the room and down the hall to the front office.

They set up the next appointment, then made their way out of the office and down to the car.

Carly drove toward home in silence. Grandma didn't say anything either. As they passed the Steak Buffet, Grandma pointed.

"Let's stop there for lunch," she suggested.

"We do have lunch things back at home."

"I messed up your birthday dinner. This is a way I can make that up to you." Grandma hesitated. "Besides, it sounds good right now."

Carly grinned and turned into the buffet parking lot. She parked, and they made their way inside.

"What is going on with you?" Grandma asked after they'd eaten in silence for a long time.

Carly wasn't sure how to answer. "I...I'm living with you now, Grandma."

"I know. But you seem down lately. I've been wondering if something is bothering you."

Carly pushed the food around on her plate, lost in thought. She didn't know if she could verbalize her feelings and she didn't know how Grandma would handle it if she told her everything.

"I guess you know I lost my job a few weeks ago." That seemed like a good place to start.

Grandma shook her head. "I can't understand that. You'd worked there for so long! Got that job straight out of college. How many years was that?"

Carly didn't hesitate. "Fifteen."

"Right! Then they let you go, no explanation, no warning. Just a pink slip and a little severance pay and that's it."

"It's a good thing I couldn't find another job. I could be here for you when you needed me."

"And I'm thankful to have you living with me and not some stranger."

Grandma didn't back down. "That isn't everything," she pressed. "You seemed to be having a hard time even before that."

Carly was puzzled. "I don't understand."

"You've been keeping to yourself. Your mom says you are irritable. You are having trouble sleeping at night, and I've noticed you don't eat much."

"I'm not hungry." Carly frowned. "Dad has sleep issues, too. You know it runs in the family."

"Carly, that isn't what I mean. Your relationship with your mom has gotten worse."

"I needed space, that's all. It's weird living at home again after having my own place for so long. Mom isn't great about giving space, either."

"While I can understand that, it seems out of the ordinary for you. You've always been happy and enthusiastic and full of life."

Carly shook her head. "You're as bad as her, Grandma. You're nagging me, trying to make me different. You don't understand me any better than she does. You think I'm a failure with life, too." Carly's voice shook with anger.

Grandma looked at her plate for a long time. When she spoke, her tone was gentle.

"I don't think you've ever failed at anything you've done. I think you are a strong, capable woman who is willing to face challenges and work through them." Grandma lifted her eyes to Carly's. "I didn't ask you to pick a fight. I want you to be happy."

Carly sagged in her seat, all her anger gone.

"I'm…I'm sorry, too, Grandma. I know you meant well. Sometimes I feel like I'm thinking through a fog. My life is good. I should be happy. But for some reason, I'm not."

Grandma smiled and reached across the table to squeeze her hand. "Is there anything I can do to help?"

"I don't know. I feel like I don't know anything anymore. I'm going through the motions of living life at this point. I wish I could find a hole, climb in it, and disappear."

Both women sat in silence again for a minute before Grandma spoke again. "Do you need to talk to someone about all this?"

"I'm talking to you right now. Does that count?"

Grandma smiled. "Yes, it does. I'm happy to listen. We'll get happy and healthy together."

Carly admired her confidence, though she didn't share it. She felt like she might never be happy again.

Chapter Seven

Saturday morning dawned hot. The lawn needed to be mowed, and Carly knew she'd better get it done early. She started as soon as she knew she was safe from violating a city noise ordinance.

Grandma came out of the house and sat on the back patio in the sun while Carly worked. The backyard was huge compared to the front yard. Once you took away the front walk, the sidewalk, and the two huge bushes in front of the house, if you turned on the lawnmower in the grass that was left, you could turn it off again and be done.

The backyard was another story. She had to mow it twice. Uncle Walter usually did it, but he'd been occupied with caring for Grandma the previous week. The yard work had been neglected. Carly raised the blade of the mower as high as it would go, and it still snared in the grass. She had to start the thing over and over and move at a snail's pace. Then she had to rake it and mow it again, shorter this time. Grandma went inside when she got too hot and brought out ice water for Carly and herself.

The neighbor came out right as Carly was finishing and waved. She leaned on the fence with her arms over the edge of the fencing and started talking the minute Carly turned off the lawn mower.

"That was a job! I have a nephew that is trying to earn some summer spending money by mowing lawns. He can do it for you sometime if you need it."

Carly shambled over to the fence. Her arms felt like they were permanently vibrating, and her palms had blisters. She should have tried to find gloves.

"I'll have to check with my Uncle Walter about that. I'm Carly, by the way."

"I'm Nadine," the lady replied. "If you decide you want him to do it, let me know. His prices are reasonable." Nadine looked up at Grandma, sitting on the back porch. "How is your grandma? I heard she was in the hospital last week. We watched the place for her while she was gone."

"She's a lot better, thanks. They never found out why she collapsed so we're going to be watching her carefully for a while."

"Well, if you ever need anything, even in the middle of the night, call me. My husband, Charles, was a paramedic for a while when we were younger. He still remembers a lot. He could be there to help until the real paramedics get there."

Carly nodded. "Thank you. I'll remember that."

"Well, I'd better let you get in out of this heat," Nadine said. She waved at Grandma, who waved back. "Talk to you later!"

That evening, Carly stood out on the back patio, admiring the results of her labor. She'd enjoyed cutting the grass ever since she was a child. The smell of the cut grass mixed with the smell of sweat and gasoline was unique to summer. She had a slight sunburn and her hands ached, but she was satisfied. Satisfied for the first time in months. The pain that had been squeezing her heart for so long had eased, and she felt content. Maybe not happy, but content.

Nadine and Charles walked up their driveway to the back door. They were sweaty and out of breath from jogging. Carly admired anyone who would get out in this kind of weather for a jog. She waved. Nadine waved back and then walked to the fence.

"Do you ever jog?"

Carly joined her at the fence line for the second time that day. "I haven't jogged for years. I don't even have the right clothes for it anymore."

Nadine laughed, a pleasant, contagious sound. "I started a few months ago. I'm not very good. Charles can't always go, and I don't like to run by myself in this neighborhood. If you'd come with me, I'd really appreciate it."

"I have to see if it's okay for me to leave Grandma, but I'll let you know."

"Promise?"

"Promise."

Carly went inside. Grandma was watching an evening game show.

"Who was out there?" Grandma asked.

"Nadine. She just got back from jogging. She asked me to join her sometime."

"Will you?"

"I don't know." Carly didn't know if she wanted to go. "I'd need clothes and shoes for it. I'm not sure I can leave you."

Grandma rolled her eyes. "I was fine living by myself until last week. Now, don't get me wrong, I'm glad you are here with me. But I don't need to be watched like a little baby. I'll be fine."

"That doesn't solve the clothes issue," Carly said. She flopped onto the couch. "I'd have to go shopping before I could start."

"Do you need something special?" Grandma asked.

"Well, I don't have shoes for it. All my shoes are either for work or everyday use. You saw those crumby clogs I wore today."

"We can go on Monday to get you some things to wear. Walter gave you money, right?"

"That was for food."

"Is that what he told you?" Grandma asked. "Did you spend it on groceries the other day?"

"Well, not all of it." Carly hesitated. They hadn't spent that much. She still had most of the money left.

"Then you can use what is left for the things you need." Grandma looked back at the television. "I need to talk with that boy. Make him clarify his instructions," she muttered to no one in particular. Then she turned back to Carly. "From now on, I'll pay for the groceries that I eat."

She sounded grumpy, and Carly had to hide a smile. Her grandma was clinging to every shred of independence she could muster.

They stayed up to watch the weather on the late news before bed. Carly slept better that night than she'd slept in months.

Chapter Eight

The heat broke late Sunday night as storms rolled through. They didn't bother Grandma. She slept through them as if nothing was happening. Carly couldn't sleep at all. She sat up with the television on and the sound turned down low watching to make sure she didn't need to find a way to take her grandma into the basement.

Once the worst of it was over, she dragged herself to bed and fell right to sleep. She overslept the next morning.

***

A man's voice cut through her dream. She opened her eyes, groggy, and sat up in bed. Will was here! She panicked and jumped out of bed. What was he doing here on a Monday?

Carly made herself presentable, then slipped into the kitchen while they were out for Grandma's walk.

She looked at the nurse's schedule on the refrigerator and groaned. Nurse visits were scheduled for Monday, Wednesday, and Friday. How had she missed that?

There was coffee in the pot from the previous morning. Carly heated a cup in the microwave. She could see evidence of the toast Grandma had fixed herself for breakfast. An extra slice sat on a plate on the table. Carly smeared jelly on it and ate it as quickly as she could so she wouldn't be caught eating when they came back.

The front door opened and closed. Grandma's and Will's voices wafted in from the living room. Carly took a deep breath and a swig of coffee, then walked into the next room.

"There she is." Grandma grinned at Carly as she settled into her chair. "I told him we were shopping today, and I didn't need to walk, but he insisted. He said they are paying him to take me for a walk."

"I said no such thing," Will protested, laughing. "I said it's my job to take you, and that the weather was pleasant today. It would be a shame not to take advantage of it."

Carly walked to the open front door and looked out. A cool breeze blew through the screen and into the room. The sky was crystal blue without a cloud in sight.

"It's an absolutely perfect day." Will's voice came from immediately behind and above her.

Carly jumped and spun around.

"I'm sorry. I didn't mean to startle you." He said. Carly had to look up to see his face.

She flushed. "It's okay. I thought you were over by Grandma." She turned back to the door.

"I guess all those storms last night blew in some better weather."

"It stormed last night?" Grandma said. "I didn't hear a thing!"

"They were really bad, Grandma." Carly turned to her. "We need to figure out a plan for what to do in bad weather. I was up most of the night worrying."

Will tilted his head to one side. "You do need a plan. The basement is the safest, but I think the hall or the bathroom would be fine in an emergency like that. I'm not sure Mrs. Terrell would be able to get back up the stairs once she went down."

He gathered up his paraphernalia. "Better get going. I'll see you again on Wednesday, Mrs. Terrell. You do those exercises I showed you. They should help your legs not ache after you've been on them for a while. Oh, and take it easy with the shopping today." He winked at Grandma as he headed to his car.

Carly shut and locked the screen door behind him. Then she flopped onto the couch and buried her face in her hands with a groan of embarrassment.

"Why didn't you wake me up before he got here?"

"You needed your rest. I didn't know that you were up most of the night. That explains a lot. I thought you were catching up from lack of sleep."

"That is the second time I was asleep when he got here, and he's only come three times." Carly groaned again.

"Why do you even care what he thinks?"

Carly gave her a look. "Really, Grandma? Do you need to ask that question?"

Grandma looked puzzled. "He's a nice young man. I'm sure he's very good looking…Oh…I see. You barely know him, sweetheart. He barely knows *you*. It's too early to worry what he thinks."

"It's too early?" Carly couldn't help sounding exasperated. "It's never too early! I'm thirty-six years old, Grandma. My chances of finding an attractive, employed, mentally sound, unmarried man my age are diminishing by the hour." She flopped back on the couch.

She sat up again after a minute and pushed herself off the couch. "I'm going to take a shower so we can get out of here."

Carly seethed with frustration at herself for not only making such a bad impression but for caring about it as much as she did.

Chapter Nine

Nadine was overjoyed when she found out that Carly wanted to run with her. They arranged to meet in the morning before it got too hot.

The following morning wasn't miserable. Carly met Nadine at the end of the driveway, and they set out. Carly needed several walk breaks, but Nadine didn't seem to mind.

"We all have to start somewhere," she assured Carly. "You are doing great. The first time I went with Charles, I had to walk almost the entire time."

When they finished, Nadine showed Carly some stretches to help her cool down. They arranged to meet a couple of days later.

"I usually run three times a week, four if I go with Charles one evening. Saturdays are a longer run day for us. You're welcome to come along if you want and you can turn around and come back sooner than we do until you work up to a longer distance."

"Do you run with Charles every Saturday?"

"Every week except the ones he has to work."

Carly shook her head. "I won't come with you, then. You guys need to do that together, and I'd be a third wheel."

"Another option is for you to go with the local running club. They meet Saturday morning at the park and run the trails," Nadine suggested.

The thought of going to a park and running with a group of total strangers made Carly physically ill. She swallowed down the sick feeling and shook her head.

"Nah. I'll figure something out."

Nadine gave her a pointed look. "Don't you dare go out alone in this neighborhood. It's unwise. Listen, I'll go with you to the running club this Saturday and introduce you to the people there. They're getting ready for a big 5K to benefit a local clinic. You'll find people at all different fitness levels, and they will be happy for you to join them. Don't run alone, okay?"

Carly nodded. "I won't. Won't that be messing up your run with Charles on Saturday?"

Nadine shrugged. "He probably has to work this week anyway. He usually does every third week. If not, I'll go twice. It'll be good for me." She grinned at Carly.

Grandma was just coming out of her room when Carly came in the back door.

"How did it go?" she asked as she picked up all the pills Carly had laid out for her to take.

"It went fine. I think I'm going to be sore tomorrow."

"When do you go again?"

"We're going again in a couple of days. Then she's going to take me to her running club on Saturday."

"Are you okay with that?"

"Nadine will be there. I know her. She'll introduce me to everyone else. I have to get over this fear of meeting new people sometime."

Carly didn't want to admit that her fear was almost debilitating. She couldn't think about it, or she'd go and hide in her room.

"You'll manage." Grandma sounded far more confident than Carly felt.

Carly could barely walk the next morning. It hurt to stand up, to sit down, to bend over. Her legs felt bruised. She couldn't sit comfortably on the hard kitchen chairs.

"I know how you feel, dearie," Grandma said with a chuckle when Carly hobbled into the living room and eased onto the couch with a groan.

Carly considered her grandma for a moment. "You probably do. I haven't done any running for so long; I've forgotten which muscles to use." She groaned again when someone knocked on the front door. Mom stood outside. She held a bucket and some cleaning rags.

"I thought I'd come over and help with the cleaning today," she announced cheerfully as she entered the house.

Carly looked at Grandma, then back at her mom.

"Carly's been doing a little every day," Grandma informed Susan. "Things are in good shape."

"Well, then we can do some extra things today since I'm here."

Carly closed the front door, her legs protesting with every movement. She didn't feel like doing anything extra today.

"The nurse will be here any minute," she said. "In fact, I thought that's who it was when you knocked."

"Well then, we'll have to do something out of the way. We won't be in the way in the kitchen, will we, Mom?" Carly's mom wasn't to be deterred. She walked into the kitchen, leaving Grandma and Carly staring at each other in the living room.

Carly was seething. "Why doesn't she ever listen to me?"

Grandma gave her head a shake and put her finger to her mouth. "She wants to help."

"It isn't helping unless it's helpful."

Carly jumped as another knock sounded at the door. This time, it was Will. She let him in, and he went straight to work.

Susan came in from the kitchen just as he began his examination.

"I thought I taught you better than to leave dishes after a meal." Both her voice and her face held a stern rebuke. "You need to take better care of your grandma."

Carly felt her face go crimson. Without a word, she turned on her heel and left the house.

"Susan, she never leaves the dishes. She was going to do them while the nurse was here." Grandma waved her hand toward Will, drawing her daughter's attention to the stranger in the room.

"Good. I'm relieved to hear that."

Grandma wasn't done. "Besides, it doesn't hurt to leave dishes for a few minutes if you don't feel like doing them right then. She's a grown woman, Susan. She can choose when she does the dishes and when she doesn't."

Will muttered that he needed something from the car and exited the front door.

Carly sat on the steps outside. Anger and embarrassment made her long for a good cry, but the tears wouldn't come. Instead, she drew her knees to her chest, her crossed arms rested on her knees. Her head hung heavy on top of her arms. She longed to disappear.

Will went to his car and fumbled around in it for a long time. Carly hadn't moved when he came walking back. He hesitated as if trying to make a decision. He sat down on the step next to her.

Carly raised her head, but she didn't look at him. Will was surprised to see that she wasn't crying. She stared out across the yard.

"I'm sorry you had to hear all that," she said, her voice modulated and controlled.

"Navigating adulthood with your parents isn't easy."

"Yeah, well my mom seems to have forgotten that I *am* an adult," Carly said with a snort. "She still thinks she can treat me like she did when I was a kid, even though I no longer live at home."

Will hesitated. "I still live at home. It's cheaper even though I pay rent and help with the food. The food is way better than I would ever fix for myself," he added with a grin.

"How's it working for you?"

"Works out pretty well. I'm not there a lot because of my jobs. When I am, I catch up on sleep or exercise. I help out as much as I can, keep my stuff picked up and my room clean, do my own laundry, that sort of thing." He sounded matter-of-fact. Carly felt her irritation easing.

"I wish it had been that way with me." She stared into the distance a moment before she spoke again. "There are expectations. I don't always know what they are so I can't meet them."

"Look, as far as caretakers go, you are one of the best ones I've ever seen. You should see some of the stuff I've encountered. Your grandma's house is clean. She's cared for and fed. You both seem to like each other. You obey the doctor's orders to a tee. I can't ask for more. It's a relief to fill out the report after I've been here. Takes me, like, two minutes, because there isn't anything to report. Keep doing what you are doing, and everything will be fine."

Carly barked a humorless laugh. "You've been here all of…four times? I haven't had a chance to mess up yet. Give it time."

"Nobody is perfect. Even if you do mess up, I'm pretty sure it won't be that bad."

Will shifted on the step and pulled out a sheet of paper. "I almost hate to change the subject, but I need to go over some changes in your grandma's medication with you. Her doctor sent a note over after her visit on Friday. We got it yesterday."

Carly nodded. "I'm glad for the subject change. Yes, the doctor mentioned some of those things. Do you want me to get the sheet from the kitchen?"

"We can go look at it in there if you're okay."

"I'm fine. Well, I'll be fine." Carly gave him a sad smile. Then she stood and walked back into the house.

Her mom was in the kitchen banging pots and pans around. Carly could tell she was upset. She didn't really want to go in the kitchen, but when she did, her mom ignored her. She carried some items back into the pantry, and she pretended not to notice Carly. Carly grabbed the medications schedule and left before her mom came back out.

Grandma smiled at her when she got back to the living room with the sheet. "She said she was going to reorganize some things and deep clean under the counters. You can put everything back the way you want it after she leaves." She winked at Carly.

Will made the changes on the medication chart and handed it back to Carly. Then he finished examining Grandma.

Carly took a deep breath and turned back to the kitchen to do those dishes. She stopped outside the door for another deep breath. Then she walked into the room. Tension crackled through the air as her mom glanced up and then returned without a word to what she was doing.

Carly and her mom worked in silence. Carly washed the two plates, knife, and coffee mug sitting in the sink. When she finished, she wrung out the cloth and stepped back to see how her mom was doing.

"Thank you for cleaning in there," Carly managed. She wanted to scream at her mom. She wanted to tell her how belittled she'd felt and how her mom's words hurt. But Mom would never admit to anything. Carly knew she felt like she'd been wronged far worse than the hurt she'd inflicted. They'd had this fight before.

"I started to clean it last week but found a lot of roaches. I stopped cleaning it because I thought Uncle Walter might need to spray," Carly continued.

Still, her mom remained silent. She removed a stack of cookie sheets and carried those into the pantry. When she came back into the room, she stopped at the pantry door.

"I deserve an apology," she spat at Carly. "I was appalled at how disrespectfully you treated me back there, especially in front of company."

Carly swallowed down the angry retort that threatened to escape. She met her mom's eyes without backing down, though all she wanted to do was go and hide from her again.

"I didn't do or say anything to you, Mom. If you want an apology, you'll have to get one from Grandma." Her eyes never left her mom's. Her voice remained steady and low. "I've done the dishes. I'm ready to help you with whatever cleaning you were wanting to get done."

Her mom brushed past her, back to the cupboard. "I prefer to work alone right now if you don't mind."

Carly nodded. "That's fine. I was dreading that job anyway, so thanks for doing it for me. I'll be in the other room if you need anything." Then she turned and went back to her room.

Will and Grandma were on their walk. Neither of them saw Carly walk up the hall. No one knew she threw herself on her bed, buried her face in her pillow, and screamed until her throat hurt.

Carly hid in her room until after Will and Grandma came back. She got them water and saw Will to the door. Mom still wouldn't talk to her. She left Grandma watching television in the living room and returned to her room.

Around noon, she heard Mom and Grandma talking again. She stood next to the door to listen.

"I don't deserve to be treated that way, Mom."

"I didn't treat you any way. I pointed out the facts. Carly does a good job with her work and she is capable. She is able to choose when she does her work and doesn't need you to tell her to do things. That's all I said. You chose to get angry at me about that." Grandma didn't raise her voice.

"This is why I haven't been over here more often. All you ever do is criticize what I do and how I do it."

Grandma was quiet for a long time. "I didn't criticize you for anything. You are blowing this out of proportion."

"That's it. I'm done. I've done my part, and you don't appreciate it. Fine. You can figure things out with Carly and do it however you want. Without me."

Carly heard the front door open. Her mom spoke again.

"You need to tell Walter that you have a roach problem in the kitchen. I cleared everything out, so he'll have an easier time getting at it. Carly will have to organize the pantry. She won't listen to me if I tell her how to do it anyway."

Then the front door slammed. Mom was gone.

Chapter Ten

Carly and Grandma ate lunch in silence. The emotions of the morning had taken their toll, and both women were tired. Carly picked at her food. She didn't feel like eating, though she knew her body needed the food. She pushed her plate back, food only half-eaten, and leaned her arms on the table.

"Some things occurred to me this morning. I'm more like my mom than I want to admit."

Grandma raised an eyebrow. "Oh? How so?"

"She interacted with you just like I interact with her."

"Hmm, I'm not sure I agree," Grandma said. "I'd say she interacted with me just like she interacts with you. The difference is I've had years of practice standing up to her."

Carly looked puzzled. "I don't understand. You two don't get along most of the time. I've known that my whole life. She and I don't get along either."

"Have you considered that the discord might not be coming from you? Today, I watched you walk away from your mom. Twice. I listened as you refused to engage in her fight."

"I don't know. I'm not always that calm." Carly shook her head and looked back down at her plate.

"You are much more like your father. He gets along with her. He lets her have space to do her thing, but he stands up to her when he can't tolerate her behavior. I've watched him do it many times. You have a disadvantage in that you are her daughter. She feels like she can push you around.

"Besides, I think things would be different if your grandpa had lived longer. She resisted me, but he could talk to her, get her to see other perspectives, influence her for good. He died when she was only a girl. After that, she was angry—at me, at God, at everyone in her life. She would overreact to the smallest things. I excused too much poor behavior. I let her off because she was missing her daddy, because she was becoming a woman, and because so much bad had happened that I wanted her to be happy. But she wasn't. She grew out of some of it, but not all of it. I should have stopped her wrong attitudes when I could. It's too late now." Sadness filled Grandma's eyes. She wiped a tear away from the corner of her eye as she finished.

"Grandma, is there hope for me to ever get along with her? Sometimes I feel like I can't do anything right. Like I've wasted my life, and I'm still not good enough for anyone." Now Carly was crying. She'd felt like giving up on her life and ending it in the last few weeks. The only reason she hadn't was because she was afraid it would hurt.

"I don't know, sweetheart. I hope so. Most of all, I hope you can be here with me and heal. You haven't wasted your life. You are good enough. Say that to yourself over and over. You are good enough. Your life is worth living."

Carly reached across the small table and squeezed Grandma's soft, wrinkled, boney hands. Grandma squeezed back.

"Leave the dishes. I want to show you something." Grandma pushed herself up from the table and shuffled out of the room.

Carly put her plate in the refrigerator to save for later and followed.

Grandma went up the hall to the third bedroom. Carly hadn't been in that room for years, but it hadn't changed much. Three large shelves filled to overflowing with fabric of every color and shade lined the wall. A sewing machine sat on its table against the opposite wall, as well as an ironing board with an iron that looked older than Carly. An easy chair was situated near the window at the other end of the room.

Grandma looked around the room and sighed with contentment. "This is my sanctuary," she said. She walked across the floor and settled in the easy chair. "Would you bring me that big bag sitting next to the sewing machine, please?"

Carly located the bag with the logo of a local fabric shop. She took it to Grandma who laid it out in her lap carefully and then lifted the end to look inside. She slid the contents out into her lap at the same time as she lowered the bag to the floor. Carly knelt on the floor in front of her.

The fabric was gorgeous. Carly loved it the moment she saw it. Deep blues, purples, and greens were set off with rich gold and rose.

"Those are the colors in Mom and Dad's bedroom!"

Grandma smiled and nodded. "Yes. Your mom and I picked the fabric years ago. I planned to make a quilt for the room when she redecorated it. I'd been having trouble with arthritis in my hands and feet for years. Not long after I started working on this quilt, the pain grew worse. I could barely tolerate it. I pushed on as long as I could. I'd work when the pain medicine was strongest, or on days when the weather was nice, and I didn't hurt as bad. Eventually, I had to stop."

Carly stroked the fabric and thought for a minute. "I could learn to do this." Her words were soft but confident.

"Yes, I know you could. I can show you. You can be my hands. I think it hurt your mother that I wasn't able to finish. She mentions it now and then. You know how she is.

"I've learned that when someone has hurt you, the most healing thing you can do is make an investment of time into their life. You can't desire their thanks because they probably won't even notice. You have to know that they won't change who they are or how they act at all. The only thing that will change is you. You will learn to love them because you've spent time doing something for them."

"I know I can't change her, Grandma. All I've wanted to do is get away from her. But now that I *am* away from her, I've found I brought her with me."

Grandma nodded. "That's how it normally works. But when you invest in her, you are learning to think about her in a different way."

"I need to do that. If I don't, I'm going to crack up. Or kill myself."

"And we don't want that." Grandma smiled at Carly. "We can start this afternoon. I can show you the basics, and you can do the work."

Chapter Eleven

S aturday morning dawned warm, promising a hot afternoon. When Nadine and Carly arrived at the park, a group of people stood around waiting for the group run to begin. Nadine introduced Carly to several other people. They all seemed friendly. Carly's nervous stomach began to relax.

They divided into pace groups, and everyone started off. Nadine was in a faster group that soon left Carly's behind. Carly looked around to discover she was surrounded by old women and one pregnant woman her age named Olivia.

"The doctor told me to take it easy," Olivia chirped cheerfully. "I'm running slower than I like and I run four days a week instead of six. I hope that's good enough for the doctor."

Carly choked. Running four days a week was taking it easy? She tried not to show her shock. She pasted a smile on her face and nodded agreement as they jogged.

The pace agreed with Olivia. She chattered on and on the whole time. Carly could barely keep up, and she was having trouble breathing. She was happy to listen to Olivia talk.

Olivia wasn't able to get out much. They'd waited for a while to have children. She worked from home because they needed the income. She had a little boy at home who had just turned one. There'd be about sixteen months between the two children, but she was glad because she'd read that children born close together get along better. Her husband was good to her and let her get out to run every day before he left for work. She loved that little bit of "me" time that she got. It made it much easier to deal with a toddler all day.

It seemed to occur to her that she should try to engage Carly in conversation. She turned to Carly and asked if she was married, had children, and where she worked.

Carly struggled to get the words out. "I'm not married. I'm...I take care of an elderly lady," she managed to gasp between breaths.

"Oh, wow! I admire you! I've heard that's a lot like taking care of a child, but I still don't think I could do it. An adult should know what to do and how to do it. I think I'd be annoyed that they need help." Then she started talking again about her son and all the work required to care for him.

Carly felt like she needed to defend her grandma. She wanted to explain that Grandma could take care of herself but that she needed someone to be with her in case of an emergency. Very few women in their eighties were in as good a physical condition as Grandma.

Carly realized too late that she had been daydreaming instead of listening to Olivia. Olivia had asked her a question about her nieces and nephews.

"My older brother is married and has four children. His oldest is almost a teenager, and his youngest is going into first grade this year." Carly hoped she was answering the right question.

Olivia seemed fine with the answer. She was already talking about her sister's children who were older than her own and how her niece babysat sometimes.

Carly could see the finish point ahead. The first group who'd returned had set out huge igloo coolers of ice water. Carly's feet were heavy, and her lungs burned.

Olivia's chatter changed to how thankful she was to get a drink and something to eat. Pregnancy made her hungry all the time.

Carly couldn't talk. She couldn't even grunt responses. She stumbled across the finish and collapsed onto a park bench.

Nadine was waiting at the finish with a cup of water. She sat next to Carly. "I see you met Olivia. She's quite the Chatty Cathy, isn't she?" She chuckled. "You did well! You kept up with your group, and you only started this week!"

Carly shook her head. Her breathing still hadn't slowed enough to let her talk.

"Ah, I see," said Nadine with a grin. "Don't feel bad. When I started running with Charles, I thought he was going to kill me. He'd go so fast—

at least that was how I felt at the time—that I couldn't keep up and breathe at the same time. But I learned to control my breathing. I'll help you with that. Controlling your breathing will help you pick up your pace, too."

Carly leaned back on the bench and took another drink. "How far did we run?"

"Your group did the 5K loop. You've run a 5K. Good job! Have you ever done that before?"

Carly shook her head. "I haven't run much since I was in high school."

"You'll have to register for the Lincoln Square Clinic 5K in August. I'll send you the link. They started it last year. It's a fun community race. Most of us here are planning to do it." Nadine waved her hand at the group in general.

"That sounds like fun," said Carly, her tone of voice indicating it would be exactly the opposite. "Gives me a goal. Maybe I'll stay motivated to work through all this pain."

Nadine laughed at her. "I better get you home before your muscles stiffen up and you can't stand and walk."

She stood and offered Carly her hand. Carly took it, and Nadine pulled her to her feet. Carly couldn't help but groan with the effort.

"You better do those stretches I showed you. In fact, let's do them before we sit in the car."

***

Carly mowed the lawn when she got home. It wasn't nearly as long as the week before, so it didn't take her as long. By the time she finished, Uncle Walter had arrived. He waved at her from the back porch as he entered through the kitchen door.

When Carly finished and came into the house, Uncle Walter had his head and shoulders under the kitchen counter. She stepped over him and got a glass of water for herself.

"Hey, there!" he said. Then he backed himself out of his tight spot and sat cross-legged on the floor. "There are some breakfast burritos that Ellen made in the fridge. Mom already had one."

"Great! I'm starved!" Carly exclaimed and headed for the refrigerator. The burritos were still warm. She grabbed a plate full of them and sat at the table to polish them off.

"A little hungry, are we?" Uncle Walter said with a chuckle.

"Yeah! Kind of unusual for me. I met the neighbor lady and went for a run and then mowed the grass before I got cleaned up. I feel like my front side is trying to gnaw through to my backside."

"Thanks for doing the yard, by the way. You don't have to do it. I was going to mow it first thing when I got here. But I appreciate you mowing it for me."

"I don't mind. I've always loved cutting the grass. I can do it if it will help you."

"It *would* help me. A lot. I have several things I need to fix for your grandma as well as keep up with things at home. Right now, I have to see if I can figure out where these nasty little bugs are hiding out and spray for them."

Carly shuddered. "Good luck with that and thank you. I hate finding them when I get up in the morning."

Uncle Walter grinned at her and tucked himself back under the counter. Carly finished her food and then went back to clean up. She and Grandma had plans for this afternoon.

Chapter Twelve

" You'll have to pick out the seam. You have a right side of that square sewed to a wrong side of that one." Grandma pointed to the squares in question.

Carly groaned. "I'm learning to hate this seam ripper." She hunched over her work and picked out the tiny stitches. When they were out, she heaved a big sigh, changed the square, and tried again.

They'd spent the morning cutting more of the pieces she would need. Then Grandma had shown her how to sew them together using simple technics. Carly still couldn't make out the pattern of what she was sewing, but every moment she came closer to that goal.

"All the sun and the out of doors is doing you good," Grandma remarked as Carly worked.

Carly glanced up at her, puzzled. "What do you mean?"

"You're smiling more than you did a few days ago. You're sleeping better at night, too."

Carly blushed. "You noticed, eh?" She gave Grandma a sheepish grin and then looked back down at her work.

"Yes, I've noticed. Besides, I like being the first one up in the morning."

Carly straightened and stretched her back. "I think I've worked long enough for one day. How 'bout we finish for tonight and I go make us some supper."

Grandma nodded. "I need to get up and move around, anyway."

Carly put her tools away and set the squares in the order Grandma had shown her, so she'd know where to begin the next time she worked on it.

Then she stood and walked over to the door. She stopped in front of the shelves.

The shelves needed a good dusting. Cobwebs hung across the front of them. But each shelf was carefully organized, most by color, some by project with the magazine or book containing the pattern on top of the stack. Other shelves held boxes with fabric scraps in them.

"Do you have other projects you started but weren't able to finish?" Carly asked, looking back at Grandma.

Grandma stopped next to Carly. "I have fabric here for a quilt I was going to make for Walter and Ellen, but I was never able to start it." She patted one of the stacks. "This one was fabric I'd saved for a quilt I found in a magazine once. I loved the pattern and how the colors worked together, but I never got around to doing it. I saved up scraps for a string quilt. I put them in these boxes. The other boxes hold squares that I cut from scraps leftover from clothing I sewed for my children when they were young."

Carly looked over the shelves. So many dreams, hopes, and plans stacked on them. It reminded her of her own life.

"I need to come in here and clean and dust," she remarked, absentminded. Then she turned and left the room, lost in thought.

Grandma followed her up the hall and into the kitchen. The stench of the pesticide Uncle Walter used earlier in the day still hung heavy in the air. They'd avoided the room except to run in for things like getting a drink of water or grabbing some leftovers for lunch. Uncle Walter had left the back door and window open, and they'd closed the pantry door. The smell had dissipated but hadn't completely disappeared.

Carly closed the back door while Grandma sank into one of the kitchen chairs for a short rest.

"How do you deal with all of those unfinished things staring at you on those shelves?" Carly asked as she pulled the casserole she'd baked for supper out of the oven.

"I don't think about it," Grandma said with a short laugh.

"Things like that bother me. It's another reminder of how I've failed at something." Carly felt strange admitting it. "I rarely start things because I'm afraid I won't finish. I should have left my job long ago to search for something better, but I didn't because I was afraid I'd be rejected and end up with no job at all. I'm afraid to try the things I dream about because I might not be able to achieve them. I stopped dreaming. It's easier that way."

Grandma sat, thoughtful. "Those stacks of unfinished things aren't a sign of failure to me. That's why they don't bother me. They are a sign that my life changed, and I had to change the things I enjoy doing. I wish I could have finished them. But it would be far more practical for me to think about giving them away than worrying about what I couldn't get done, worrying about circumstances outside my control."

Carly set the table and filled their plates. Then she sank into the other kitchen chair.

"What dreams do you have?" Grandma asked.

"I haven't thought about them in so long. I'm not even sure I have the same dreams anymore," Carly admitted.

"You should think about it. I'd love to hear them."

Carly didn't want to think about the dreams she'd lost. Coping with life was easier when she didn't.

Chapter Thirteen

The quilt project took over the whole house, spread from the back bedroom to the living room. Carly frantically tried to get it organized before Will arrived on Monday.

"Don't worry about it, Carly," Grandma said. "Will won't care."

"I want it to be neat," Carly insisted.

"It *is* neat. At least it looks neat to me."

Will arrived before Carly could finish. He surveyed the room with admiration.

"My great-aunt used to do this stuff," he said. "These colors here are great. I love how it looks."

Grandma looked at Carly with a self-satisfied expression on her face. "I told you he wouldn't mind."

Carly rolled her eyes and started into the kitchen.

"Do you have any of it finished?"

Grandma waved Carly back into the living room. "Show him what you've finished."

Carly walked to one of the stacks. "The pattern is a little complicated for me. I've been spreading the blocks out on the couch to make sure I'm still doing the next part of the pattern correctly. But here. These are the finished blocks. You have one that looks like this." She laid the first type of block on the couch cushion. "And another that looks like this." She laid the second type next to it. "When they are finished the pattern looks like this." Carly showed Will the pattern in the open quilt book.

Will let out a low whistle. "This is amazing. It's like a painting, only with fabric. My aunt didn't make them like this. Her's were, ah, well, less complicated. Mostly scrap quilts."

Carly gave a short laugh. "I should have started on something less complicated. But Grandma is helping me. She knows what to do."

"Carly is my hands so this project can get finished. She's doing well, especially considering she's never done anything like this before."

Carly replaced the stacks in order again and turned to leave the room.

"It'll be fun to watch your progress." Will's enthusiasm was palpable.

Carly flushed and nodded. "It'll probably be spread all over the living room for a while. The progress will be hard to miss."

***

The following morning dawned cloudy and gray. Just about the time Carly met Nadine for their run, it started to rain. At first, a few sprinkles spit at them here and there. But after a few minutes, the rain was falling fast and hard.

"Takes dedication to run in the rain," Carly grumbled.

Nadine laughed. "Charles won't miss a run, even in snowstorms. He has special shoes he uses. He refuses to buy a treadmill. Says they are a waste of money."

Carly shook her head in disbelief. "I don't think I'm that dedicated."

"Give it a few weeks and months. The running gets into your blood, and you find you need to do it, rain or shine. Besides, we're going to get sweaty anyway."

"Did you run before you and Charles got married?"

"Not really. I mean, I did run now and then with friends, but not on any regular basis."

"Do you all have any children?"

"No. We haven't been able to have any. Charles has a couple from his first marriage. We were older when we got married. I'd had some health problems when I was younger, and my doctor told me I might not be able to conceive."

"How did you and Charles meet?" Carly asked. She hesitated, then laughed. "Talking is distracting. It helps me not notice how miserable I am with every step I take."

Nadine chuckled along with her. "I don't mind talking about it! We met when his first wife was in the hospital. She had a rare form of rheumatoid arthritis that was attacking her heart muscle. She deteriorated before our eyes. Charles was devastated by it.

"I worked in the finance office and dealt with insurance claims and adjustments. Charles came in now and then to discuss their account. He was heartbroken when she died. He kept coming in to pay the bill. I told him he could mail it, but he said that he preferred having something of the routine he'd had when she was alive. We'd start talking about his wife, about his job, about his children. One day, several months later, he made the last payment and asked me out to lunch.

"We had such a nice time that he asked me to lunch the following week. Then he asked me to come with him to his book club, then his running club. Mind you, I hadn't run much in years. I felt a lot like you have the past couple weeks. But I wasn't about to let him know that! I soldiered on and tried not to let him see how much pain I was in.

"One day, when we'd been doing things together for two years, he told me that he'd realized he couldn't live without me in his life and asked me to marry him. We were married a couple of months later in a quiet ceremony."

"What did his children think?" Carly asked.

"They weren't thrilled at first. They were angry at him for finding another woman. They were angry at me for 'stealing' him from their mother. His youngest daughter came around first. She had a guidance counselor in high school who helped her through it. She was able to convince her brothers and sister that we weren't evil.

"Once we came through those initial struggles, I loved joining his family. I'd always dreamed of marrying young. That didn't happen. When I was just out of college, I was told I'd never be able to have children. Now, not only am I married, I have children and grandchildren. I never knew I could be this happy."

Carly flushed. She'd had the same dreams - marriage, children, her own home. The older she got, the more she assumed her dreams would never come true.

They had returned to their driveways. The rain had let up while they were running but now was coming down in earnest.

"I better get in to Grandma," Carly said. Rain streaked down her hair and face. She started up her driveway then turned back to Nadine. "How old were you when you got married?"

"I was a month away from my fortieth birthday. I'd given up all hope, then suddenly I had everything." She paused as if contemplating a wonderful memory. Then she looked at Carly, still smiling. "See you in a couple of days. Don't forget to stretch!"

Chapter Fourteen

Carly would happily have talked herself out of meeting the running club on Saturday. The weather grew hotter and more humid as the weekend approached. The pain from Grandma's arthritis intensified until she could hardly move. Both women were up before sunrise that morning. Carly did everything she could to make her grandma more comfortable. Finally, after a call to the doctor's office exchange, she gave Grandma a dose of the strong pain pills, the ones they'd been working to wean her off for the last several weeks.

As the medicine began to work, Grandma relaxed in her chair and Carly, still in her pajamas, sank onto the couch.

"Aren't you planning to go for a run this morning?" asked Grandma, her words slurred as sleep approached.

"I was going to stay here with you to make sure you are okay."

"You should go." Despite her drowsiness, Grandma's voice held a command. "You need to get out sometimes. Nothing to do here if I'm asleep." Her eyes closed. With the very next breath, she was snoring.

Carly sighed. She knew she ought to go. She thought of Nadine and how she would ask if Carly had gone. She thought of Olivia and all her chatter. Maybe she wouldn't be there today because of the weather. Was it good for a pregnant woman to run in this heat and humidity?

Carly shoved herself to her feet, went to her room, and dressed for the run. She slipped out the kitchen door and sat on the patio step to tie her shoes. Feet dragging, she got into her car. She felt sick to her stomach at the thought of going there alone. It had been fine last week. But Nadine had been there.

Before she could change her mind, she started the car and backed out of the driveway.

Carly was amazed that so many people would come out in the heat for a run. The group this week was larger than it had been the week before. Water coolers were set up, and people were getting drinks in preparation.

Carly got out of the car and locked it. Then she stood there, looking at the keys, fumbling them around in her fingers. Terror gripped her stomach. It would go away if she would just get back in that car and drive home. She couldn't do it. She couldn't walk up to that group of virtual strangers.

"Carly? Is that you?"

A man's voice behind her startled Carly out of her mental quandary. She whirled around. Will stood in front of her on the sidewalk.

"Will? I didn't know you were in the running club." Carly couldn't believe the relief that washed over her at the sight of someone familiar.

"Not every week," he replied. "I have to work a lot of weekends. When I don't, I come here and run with them. Well, most times anyway. I didn't know you came either."

Carly shook her head. "I haven't come, not by myself. This is the first time. Last week I came with our next-door neighbor, Nadine."

"I didn't know Nadine was your neighbor! That's cool! Her husband, Charles, is a running legend in this group. You ready for this?"

Carly tucked the keys into her pocket. Then they walked together toward the rest of the group that was getting itself organized into smaller pace groups. Carly saw her pace group from the prior week. Olivia was there, already talking and laughing with an older woman. Carly held back.

"I guess I'm ready for this. I haven't been running for long." She hesitated as she approached the group.

"You want to run with me?" Will asked.

"I'm slow. Very slow. Last week I had trouble keeping up with the slowest group. A pregnant woman was better at it than I was. Snails finish faster."

Will chuckled. "I'm sure it isn't as bad as that. Even so, I haven't been for a run in, well, in longer than I care to admit. I can use to ease into this. How 'bout it?"

"Okay, but don't laugh at me if I can't keep up with your long legs." Carly looked up at the tall man standing in front of her.

His eyes met hers. They held a smile. "Ready? We can start whenever you want."

They set off, just the two of them. Carly got through those first five minutes of running when her lungs and legs burned and when she felt the most like quitting. Once her body stopped trying to dissuade her from this form of torture, she settled into a comfortable pace and kept up with Will without any trouble. Even though his legs were long, he didn't seem eager to run faster.

They ran in silence at first. Carly was comfortable. She didn't need to fill the silence with chatter. The silence was companionable. Will was the first to break it.

"How is your grandma this morning?" he asked.

"Not great. She was in so much pain that the normal pills did nothing to alleviate it. I had to call the doctor's exchange. They said for her to take one of the stronger pills. She was sleeping when I left."

"That's the great thing about having her on something less potent. Makes the strong stuff pack a bigger punch when she does take it. I hope she feels better soon. It has to be this weather. Are you signing up for the Lincoln Square Clinic 5K in August?"

"Nadine thinks I should. I haven't done it yet, but I plan to. Are you doing it?"

"I have to. My sister is the one who organized it the first time. If I didn't participate, she'd probably disown me."

"What's your family like?"

"I'm the oldest in my family, and as of this afternoon, I'm going to be the only unmarried one. My sister is getting married."

"In this weather? Poor thing!" Carly couldn't imagine wearing a wedding dress in this humidity.

"Yeah, well, she's happy to be tying the knot. They'd have married months ago if Mom hadn't wanted the whole huge shindig."

"Do you have something to do for the wedding?" Carly asked.

"I'm an usher. I'm also the proud brother who stands there looking threateningly at the groom, reminding him that he better treat my sister right *or else.*"

Breathless from running, Carly gasped out a laugh. "I can see my brother doing that. You have to be sure to wear sunglasses, even indoors. It looks more threatening."

"Yeah, well, I like the guy. He has that going for him. Alice is a nurse, too. They met a couple of years ago. I wasn't sure about him at the time. She seemed to like him, but I was afraid he was leading her on. Then, all of a sudden, he popped the question. He has a kid he adopted. In fact, I think he and his little girl live not far from where your grandma lives."

"Really?" Carly was surprised. She didn't know people were intentionally moving into that neighborhood.

"This is going to seem a little random and sudden to you, but would you be my plus one at the wedding today? I was going to go alone, but I'd rather go with you."

Carly hesitated. "Grandma isn't doing well."

"Oh, yeah. I forgot about that." Will's face fell. "Don't worry about it then. I understand."

"Why don't I check with my Uncle Walter? He usually comes over on Saturdays. If he's going to be there anyway, I don't need to be there. I can call him when we get back to the cars and let you know for sure. I think I'd enjoy going with you if it will work out." Carly smiled up at the tall man loping along beside her. She suddenly felt shy.

"Sounds good. If you come, they will be so shocked they might forget all about Alice getting married." He winked at her, and then laughed out loud, a guffaw that echoed in the trees around them. Carly couldn't help but join him.

They reached the cars and Carly got her water bottle out for a long drink. She didn't feel as miserable at the end of the run this week as she had last week. She did the stretching Nadine had shown her. By that time, her breathing had slowed to the point where she could talk on the phone without sounding like she was dying.

Uncle Walter was planning to come by that afternoon. He said he'd be glad for her to get out and not rush back.

Carly turned to Will when she'd hung up with Uncle Walter. "I can come if you still want me."

Will's face broke into a huge grin. "Yes, I do. Well, then, I'll be by to pick you up a little after noon. It's dressy but not formal. I'm wearing a suit."

Carly nodded. "Okay. I can do that. I'll see you then." She waved and got into the car to head home. She needed to get that grass cut before it got too hot, and she needed time to "primp and fuss" as Grandma said.

She had a date! She hadn't been on a date in years. Her stomach fluttered, but this time she didn't mind.

Chapter Fifteen

"How do I look?" Carly stopped in front of Grandma and gave a spin. She felt awkward walking in the heels she was wearing, and she'd opted for an up-do with her hair because of the heat. Her dress was from the office party last Christmas. She left off the long-sleeved sweater she'd worn in the winter.

"You look lovely. He'll be proud to be with you."

Carly heard someone knock on the front door. She could see Will's car in the driveway.

"You call if you need anything," Carly insisted as she went to get the door. "I'll be home as quick as I can."

"I'm here," Uncle Walter called from the kitchen. "I'll be here the whole time. Have fun and don't worry about her!"

Carly opened the front door.

Will stood there waiting in a dark suit, crisp white shirt, and blue striped tie. Carly's heart fluttered, and her stomach flopped. He was gorgeous. Carly felt her face flushing with the thought.

"You look nice," he said, "which is kind of an understatement."

"So do you."

Will leaned in the door and waved at Grandma. "I don't know when I'll have her home, but it'll be sometime this evening."

"She's an adult. She can stay out as long as she needs." Grandma waved them away. "You kids have fun!"

They walked to the car, and Will opened the passenger side door for Carly.

She climbed in, smoothed her skirt, and tried to settle the nerves in her stomach. Will got in and started the car.

"The wedding isn't far from here. First Baptist Church. You might know the place."

Carly nodded. She did know the place. Grandma had gone there for a long time. She remembered attending Vacation Bible School there as a child.

"Then they're having the reception at this local restaurant, The Balustrade. Parker and Alice went there when they were dating or something, and Parker did a favor for the guy that runs it. They've rented out the place for this evening and are holding the reception there."

Carly gave a low whistle. "Wow. They must know the right people to get that kind of treatment."

Will laughed. "I'm sure they are paying for it, but still, you're right. Parker does know some of the right people around town. You'd never know how connected he is when you hear him talk."

They rode in silence until they pulled into the church parking lot.

"We already did a lot of the pictures this morning. Man, is my mom going to be shocked when I walk in with a girl." Will parked the car and then turned to look at Carly. "That came out wrong. I'm really glad I'm here with you. I think my family has given up on me ever getting married, or even dating for that matter. They're going to be happy to see you."

"No pressure then, eh?" said Carly with a laugh.

"Nope, no pressure. I'm planning to thoroughly enjoy the day. With you." Will reached out and squeezed Carly's hand. "Ready?"

They had arrived long before the wedding was to start, but quite a number of people stood in the foyer and around the auditorium. Will showed Carly the place he was supposed to sit once the wedding began.

"Come on," he said. "I want you to meet my mom and sisters."

"Isn't that bad luck or something?" Carly asked.

"I don't think so. Parker already saw the bride when we got pictures taken. I'm pretty sure it's okay for you to see her." He led the way out of the auditorium.

He stopped in front of a classroom and rapped on the closed door with his knuckles. He opened it when they heard a soft "Come in!" from inside.

Carly saw the bride first. She looked beautiful, blond hair swept up with braids and curls, ribbons and pins. A simple sheath dress in textured satin fell to the floor with a small train and a cowl in the back.

Carly stared at Alice. She was different from Will—shorter, blonde instead of dark hair, more like an athlete than a runner. She struggled to see the family resemblance until she saw Will's mom. Then the dots connected. All three shared the same square jaw and pointed chin, the same square forehead, and the same gray-blue eyes. A third woman walked into the room. She shared similar facial features to Alice but had Will's dark hair.

"Mom, Alice, Grace, this is Carly. Carly, my mom and sisters," Will said.

Carly smiled at them and nodded. All three women stood, frozen in place, a look of shocked disbelief registered on their faces.

"Will, did you let your sister know a month ago when the RSVPs were due that you were bringing an extra person?" Will's mom finally spoke.

Carly looked up at Will, curious to hear his answer.

"He did, Mom. It's okay," Alice said.

"You did?" Carly asked, surprised. "A month ago, you told her you were bringing a date, but you didn't ask me until today?"

Will's grin turned sheepish, and he started to run his fingers through his hair when all three of the other women in the room called out a protest, and he stopped.

"Well, I...I wasn't sure how keen you'd be to go out with a guy you'd just met. It took me a while to get up the nerve to ask," Will answered with a shrug, shuffling his feet and stuffing his hands in his pockets.

Carly shook her head. "I don't know if that's a compliment or a sign of desperation."

Will's mom crossed the room and took her by the hand. "It's a compliment. Believe me. He'd rather go to weddings alone than go with a girl he doesn't like, even if he was set up with someone."

"That I can understand," Carly agreed. "It's happened too many times for me to count."

"I know! Right?" Will said.

Grace interrupted. "Have any of you seen Jasmine? She was supposed to be waiting in here with us."

"I'm here," called a voice from the next room. "Daddy got me some books to color."

A tiny girl in a frilly white dress entered the room. Grace visibly relaxed.

"That's great, honey. Let's bring those in here so I can see you." The two left the room and came back a moment later with some books and colored pencils. She settled the girl at a table and then turned back to the group.

"We'll have to talk more later," Will said. "I have to get out there and be an usher. See you ladies in a few minutes." He offered his arm to Carly.

She took it, hesitant, and walked with him back to the auditorium. Will led her up the aisle to their seat. Carly sat down, and Will sat down next to her.

"When did you decide I was going to be your 'plus one' for today?"

Will flushed and looked down at his hands. "Pretty much the first time I met you." He looked up at her with a half grin. "Sorry it took so long to actually ask."

"That day when I came out all ratty looking and tired and hid from you all morning, that's when you decided to ask me out." Carly stared at the front of the church instead of looking at Will.

"That isn't quite how I remember it," Will said. "You were cute and nervous. Then you hid in the kitchen the whole time. I was disappointed. I wanted to talk to you more. I decided I'd see if you would come with me to the wedding. I told Alice I was bringing someone. It took me a while to get up the nerve to ask you." The sheepish smile was back on his face.

"I'm glad you asked." Carly cut Will a look out of the corner of her eye. "Really glad."

Will smiled down at her. He took her hand again and squeezed it. "Gotta go. I'll be back before long."

The pianist started to play. Will stood and walked to the back of the church. People began to trickle in. Carly listened to the pianist, enthralled. Her fingers flew over the piano keys. The program said 'Shondra O'Neill'.

Before Carly even realized what was happening, the doors to the auditorium were closed, and the ceremony began.

***

Later that evening, Carly and Will sat at a table at The Balustrade. The murmur of voices flowed around them. Parker and Alice milled through the group, Parker carrying a tired Jasmine with him everywhere he went.

"She had to wait a long time for Parker to come along." They'd been sitting together, quiet, watching the people around them when Will spoke.

Carly looked at Will. "She's younger than you, right?"

"Yeah. I'm oldest, then Grace, then Alice. Alice didn't meet Parker until a couple of years ago. Before she met him, she said she was married to her job."

"She's a nurse, right?" Carly wanted to make sure she remembered everything Will had already told her.

"Yes. She works in the cancer ward at the hospital. That's how she and Parker met. Parker's nephew had cancer, and she was there when he was treated." Will answered.

"Have you given up on getting married?" Carly asked, almost afraid of the answer.

"I guess I'm so busy I don't think about it much." Will said.

Carly shook her head. "I don't think I've ever been that busy." She didn't want to delve into her personal feelings with a man whom she barely knew.

"How did you get that scar on your neck?" she asked, hoping to change the subject.

"Oh, that." Will reached up and touched the scarred skin. "I barely remember it's there most of the time. Alice and I were goofing around by a campfire one time when we were kids. I tripped and fell in and got burned on my upper arms, chest, and neck. The doctor said it was a miracle it wasn't worse. That's probably why we both went into the medical profession."

"Wow! That's crazy." Carly looked at it. Her frank gaze didn't seem to bother him. "Did you have skin grafts?"

"Yes. Mainly on my neck where you can see it. The rest was covered in clothing and didn't get as badly burned."

The conversation moved on to other subjects and the evening passed in a blur. A few people still milled around the restaurant when Carly finally looked at her cell phone.

"It's after 10 o'clock! I need to get back!"

They said their goodbyes and left. Carly didn't want the evening to end. Will walked her to the door when they reached Grandma's house. A lamp glowed through the living room window. Will looked down at her in the light it provided. Then he lifted her fingertips and touched them to his lips.

"I haven't had such a wonderful evening in a long time," he said. "I hope we can do this again."

Carly swallowed hard and nodded. "I would like that," she said. Then she slipped into the darkened house.

Chapter Sixteen

Carly floated on the memory of that afternoon for the next several days. She hadn't been this happy in a long time.

She decided to finish her mom's quilt in time for Independence Day. With Grandma's help and a lot of seam ripping, she finished the top. Then she started putting the layers together to quilt. Grandma tried to help, but her shaky, arthritic fingers wouldn't cooperate. A few tears and a great deal of frustration later, she finally got it all smooth and put safety pins in to hold it all together. Thanks to YouTube videos, she was able to figure out how to do the quilting stitch, something else Grandma wasn't able to show her. She kept the seam ripper handy. Little by little, she got the hang of what she was doing and made progress.

Will watched the process with as much excitement as Grandma. He inspected it every time he came and exclaimed about how good it looked. Even Uncle Walter got excited about it.

Carly finished the quilting several days early. Then she spent the rest of the time figuring out how to put the binding on the edge. Once the quilt was finished, she spread it on the couch and photographed it. That task complete, she folded it and put it into a large bag by the front door. Carly thrilled with excitement and satisfaction when she saw it sitting there. She could hardly wait to see her mom's face when she opened it.

***

The family Independence Day celebration took place at Carly's parent's house. She and Grandma drove there mid-morning and planned to stay until Grandma got tired.

They had decided to wait until after they'd eaten and cleaned up from the meal. Carly insisted Grandma should give it to her. She didn't want Grandma to say anything about her work on it.

By the time they'd finished everything, it was late afternoon, and Grandma was beginning to tire from the long day. Carly knew they'd need to leave soon after giving the quilt so Grandma could get home and rest. She went out to the car and got the bag out of the back seat. Mom was in the kitchen. She hurried the bag over to Grandma, and they slid the finished quilt out onto Grandma's lap.

Susan came into the room a few minutes later. She noticed the quilt laying on Grandma's lap almost immediately. Carly held her breath in anticipation of her mom's excitement. She leaned forward, all her muscles tense. For once, she felt like she'd done something right.

Uncle Walter and Dad were talking in the easy chairs across the room. Aunt Ellen, Dale, and Jessie were looking through photos of her grandchildren on Aunt Ellen's phone.

"Oh! You finally finished that old thing. Look at the outdated colors on it! I can't believe I ever chose them. You got it done a little late. Richard and I picked out new paint and curtains for our room this week. We might even get new carpet in there. That quilt won't even match anymore." She finished with a laugh.

The entire room fell silent. Carly felt her chest tighten and she struggled to breathe. She wanted to cry, to scream, but nothing would come.

Mom leaned in closer to the quilt. "Your eyesight is really going, Mom. This is all bunchy, and the seams don't line up. Or did Carly make it?" She glanced in Carly's direction. "You should leave the quilt making to your grandma and worry about all that housecleaning you don't need my help doing."

Carly felt like she was gasping for air. Everyone in the room was staring at her. Her face flushed, but her legs refused to move and carry her out of the room, away from the stares, the pain.

Mom wasn't done. "Oh, by the way, we got new paint and curtains for your room, too, Carly. It's outdated, too. I hope that's okay. We'll pack up your things and put them in the garage, and you can get them when you want them." She hesitated and glanced around. "I think I left my drink in the kitchen. Better go get it before I get settled." She left the room.

Without a word, Carly stood, gathered the quilt into the bag, and carried it out to the car. She shook. Anger, frustration, and hurt washed over her in waves. How could she have been so stupid to think that this poorly crafted gift would change her relationship with her mom for the better? She stood by the car and attempted to collect herself before she went back inside.

"Carly, the quilt is beautiful." Aunt Ellen's voice came from behind her, but Carly didn't turn around.

"She's right. It's bunchy and not all the seams match," Carly said. She tried to keep her voice from shaking, but she felt like she was choking on the words.

Aunt Ellen laid her hand on Carly's back. "The seams never match perfectly all the time. I saw it too. It isn't bunchy. Just needs to be washed. I love it! You did a remarkable job. I'm impressed with how well it turned out. It's your first quilt. You should be proud of it."

"If she doesn't want it, I'll take it." Jessie had come out with Aunt Ellen. "I've always loved those colors. Maybe I can talk Dale into repainting our room."

Carly turned around and took several deep breaths. Her chest was still clenched tight, and she felt on the verge of tears, but she was no longer shaking. She looked up at the two women in front of her. She couldn't smile, but she squeezed Aunt Ellen's hand where it rested on her arm and then accepted Jessie's hug.

When they got back inside, Mom wasn't in the room. Dale murmured something about how she'd gone to the bathroom and hadn't seemed to notice they were all outside. Carly went back to sit at her place on the couch. Her dad came over to sit next to her. He put his arm behind her on the couch. Carly leaned her head on his shoulder.

"I didn't pick the new paint. She did. She asked me one day last week if I liked a certain color. When I came home from work, she'd picked paint and curtains for your room and ours."

"I know, Dad. I know how she is."

"I won't let her pack up your things without you here. Don't worry. Maybe you should come over Saturday while Walter is with your grandma to pack them yourself."

"I'll do that. Thanks, Dad."

"That quilt is amazing. I'm not saying that because I have to. You did a good job on it. I'd be happy to have that quilt on our bed. A quilt my own daughter made. Not some generic thing you buy in a store somewhere that looks the same as thousands of other quilts and was made in China."

Carly believed him. Her dad was proud of her work. That made up for her mom not liking it at all. But only a little.

The long day had taken its toll on Grandma. Carly gathered their food and put everything in the car. They said their goodbyes and left.

Grandma was the first to break the silence during the car ride home.

"I'm sorry, Carly, so very, very sorry. I can't believe she did that to you."

"Yeah, well, I can. I should have seen it coming. Here I let myself get my hopes all up that for once she'd approve of something I'd done, that she'd like it. One thing is for sure. Mom is predictable and consistent." Carly shuddered, her agony written all over her face.

"It isn't your fault. You did good work."

"Jessie wants it. I think Aunt Ellen does, too, though she'd never admit it."

"See there! It isn't ugly and outdated like your Mom said! It's beautiful, a real work of art."

"I know, Grandma. I mean, my head knows. But my heart is still hurt," Carly said.

"I think you should keep it. Then you'll have the first quilt you ever made," Grandma suggested.

"I don't want to keep it. I want to give it to someone and never see it again. Every time I look at it, I'll remember what a failure I am."

"You aren't a failure, Carly. Far from it. But I understand if you don't want to keep it. You can give it away if you want. Someone else will love it for the work of art that it is." Grandma settled back in her seat as if that was the end of the matter.

That night, after Grandma was settled in bed, Carly longed to be able to have a good cry and be done with it. She'd been happy. The depression she'd struggled with for so long had been going away. She was enjoying new people and doing new things.

In one selfish act, her Mom had taken all that away. Carly wished with all her heart that her mom didn't have that power over her, but she did. As she lay in bed that night, Carly gathered the quilt Grandma had made her and wrapped it around her, as though she was wrapping herself in her grandma's arms. Then the tears came. Carly cried herself to sleep.

Chapter Seventeen

Will came to check on Grandma the next day. Carly was happy to see him, but the hurt from the previous day was fresh and raw. She slipped outside to the back patio to let him work with Grandma alone. For the last couple weeks, she'd been hanging around. The three of them would talk and laugh while he checked Grandma. She heard them leave the house and come back a few minutes later. She heard them talking, Will's deeper voice and Grandma's soft, higher one. She heard laughter and cringed. She didn't know how anyone could laugh. She wanted to be angry at them for laughing, but she couldn't. The hurt was there, throbbing, refusing to go away, reminding her of all that she did wrong.

The back door opened and closed and then Will, in his scrubs, sat down next to her on the back step.

"You're going to get your pants dirty," Carly said. Her voice held no emotion.

"Your grandma told me what happened. I can't even tell you how mad it makes me to hear it. I'd like to go tell the woman off. My mom wouldn't do anything like that, but if she did, I would probably yell at her and then never speak to her again. You are a better person than I am, Carly."

"Don't get angry at her on my behalf. You haven't been around her." Carly swiped at the tear that slid down her cheek.

"Yeah, well maybe that's a good thing. You don't...You don't treat people that way, especially family."

"Thanks, Will. It means a lot to me to hear you say that." Carly looked up at him and tried to smile. It came off as more of a grimace. She buried her face in her arms and sobbed.

Will hugged her and rubbed her back. When she was done, he offered her a kleenex. "Just happened to have this with me."

This time Carly's smile and laugh were real. "Just happened, eh? Did you think I was sitting out here crying?"

"I didn't know what to think. I came prepared." He grinned at her and handed her another one.

"I also came prepared for something else. You see, I never got Parker and Alice a wedding gift. I didn't know what to get them. They've both been keeping house for a while, and they had all the usual stuff you need. I wanted to get them something they'd use, but that would be special and unique.

"I came prepared today to beg you to make me a quilt to give them. They would love something like that. Actually, I think they would love the quilt you made for your mom. But since I didn't think that was still available, I was going to see if you'd make me another one for them. I'm going to pay you for it." He pressed several bills into Carly's hand. "You can't refuse the money. You deserve to be paid for all that work."

Carly looked at the money in her hand and then back up at Will, forgetting all about her tear-stained and blotchy face.

"It's outdated and bunchy, and the seams don't line up."

"It isn't outdated or bunchy, at least not that I could see. I'm not sure what you mean about the seams, but I think it's beautiful. Your Grandma and everyone else agree. And it doesn't matter what your mom thinks. She's got a problem with her head." Will reached up and wiped the tears off Carly's face. His hand lingered on her chin. "You did a really great thing for her. You are a wonderful person, Carly."

Carly looked down. She didn't think she was all that great. What kind of person couldn't get along with their own mom? But his words reassured Carly in a way that the rest of the family's words could not. They had to be positive and encouraging. Familial relationships demanded it. But he didn't. He had no long-term investment in her life demanding he say things to make her feel better.

"You can have the quilt. I'm happy someone will enjoy it, and I don't want to have it here as a reminder. But I hate to take your money. I can just give it to you."

"Nah, it's worth the money to me. In fact, I'm getting off easy only giving you that much." He nodded toward the money in her hand. "Don't ever go online and google to find out how much handmade quilts cost these days." With a grin and a wink, Will stood and went inside.

Carly followed, still clutching the money in her hand. She showed him the bag with the quilt where she'd dropped it like a poisonous snake the night before.

Will looked like a little kid who'd won a prize at the fair. "I can hardly wait to give this to them! I told them their gift wasn't finished yet. They're going to love it."

His enthusiasm was a healing balm on Carly's hurt. The tightness in her chest eased. "Thank you."

"No, thank *you*!" Then he was out the door and gone with a wave.

Carly still clutched the money in her hand. She held it out to Grandma. "This is yours, I think. You bought all the materials and spent the time cutting it out."

"No, it's yours," Grandma insisted. "You did most of the work on it."

"How 'bout we put it in a special place and it will be our fun money?" Carly suggested. "That way, if we want to stop and eat out on the way home from the doctor's or if we want to pick up a treat at the supermarket, we can use that money and not what is budgeted for groceries."

"Excellent idea." Grandma beamed at Carly. "Now, I think I need a nap before lunch. I'm still worn out from yesterday."

Carly took the money to her room and tucked it into an envelope. Then she put that envelope in her purse. They had a doctor's appointment in a few days. She'd take Grandma out to eat afterward. She knew Grandma would enjoy it. Maybe by then, she would, too.

Chapter Eighteen

C arly dreaded going back to her parent's house on Saturday, but she dreaded her mom going through her things and packing them even more. As soon as she had gone for her run, cut the grass, and showered, she drove to her parent's house.

When she arrived, her mom wasn't even home. Carly tried not to show her dad how relieved she felt, but she wasn't ready to face her mom. Not yet.

"I found some boxes you could use," Dad said, pointing to the boxes stacked on the bed.

Carly nodded. "Thanks, Dad. That's a huge help."

Emptying her dresser and desk was easy. She'd already taken most of her clothes to Grandma's house. Carly found things she didn't remember owning, so she made a box for items to donate. She found stationary she'd used as a child, necklaces that had seemed like the coolest thing at the time, and old bottles of nail polish in wild colors that were dried up. These made their way to the trash.

The closet held shoeboxes with photos in them—from camp, birthdays, learning to ride her bike, first and last days of school each year, senior pictures and graduation. Carly found clothes hanging in the closet that she hadn't worn since high school.

Soon, she noticed the "donate" pile was larger than the pile she was keeping.

Dad came into the room a few hours later. "Do you have anything you want me to move out of your way?"

Carly pointed at the boxes filled with things to be donated. "Those can go out to my car. I'm taking them to Goodwill. After that, I'm almost done. I don't have a lot to store."

Dad picked up the first box and walked to the door. Turning back, he said, "Don't run off when you're done. There are some leftovers in the fridge from the other day. Would you like some lunch? I'd love to sit and visit with you for a while. We didn't get to talk at all on Independence Day."

Carly saw pain behind Dad's eyes. She'd never doubted her daddy loved her. "I'd like that."

She returned her attention to the boxes in front of her. She divided out the things she wanted to take to Grandma's. Then she began packing the rest into the boxes that remained. One of the shoe boxes fell open. A photo of Carly and her mom rested on the top. Carly remembered that day clearly—Mother's Day the year she'd turned eight. She and Dale were sitting on Mom's lap. Neither fit very well, and they were all laughing about it. Carly picked up the picture and looked at it. She smiled. They'd been so happy.

As she placed the picture back in the box, the one underneath caught her attention. The family picture had been taken a few years ago before Dale got married. Mom no longer looked happy. What had happened?

Carly heard Dad's footsteps down the hall. She didn't look up.

"What do you have there?" Dad asked, looking over her shoulder.

Carly showed him the picture from her childhood. "We were happy back then. What happened? We aren't happy together in this picture." She lifted the newer picture from the box and held it out so he could see it.

"I've been thinking about it, and I think it's time you knew…I hadn't planned on telling you, or anyone really, about this, but I think you need to know." Dad cleared a spot on the bed and sat down. Carly sank cross-legged onto the floor.

"After Dale was born, your mom was all wrapped up in the new baby. At least that's what I thought. She had no interest in me anymore, didn't want to spend time with me or be around me. We couldn't get along, so we started couples counseling. I found out she'd been having an affair the whole time. Her disinterest in me wasn't because of the new baby. She had another man.

"I was trying to make our marriage work. Your mom said she broke things off with the man, but she was unhappy. I told her I would give her a divorce, let her have custody of Dale. She could move on with her life and be happy. She said no, that she wanted to work on things with the two of us. We kept plugging away with the counseling and tried to be happy together. Not long after that, she found out she was pregnant with you."

"Who is my father?" asked Carly, cold terror gripping her.

"I'm your father, Carly," Dad assured her.

"No, I mean my biological father," she clarified.

"I'm your biological father. Your mom got a paternity test. You see, come to find out, your mother never stopped having that affair. She kept seeing the other man now and then the whole time we were supposed to be working on our marriage. He was a married man. He got a job in another city and asked her to move with him. He said he would live there with her part-time and travel back here to see his wife and their children." Dad looked down at his hands, clasping and unclasping them as he thought.

"She thought about it. She even traveled there with him for a business trip. She told me she was going to visit a sick aunt. In the end, she decided not to go with him. I never heard exactly what happened, but I think his wife found out about the affair.

"Your mom gave birth to you, all the while thinking you were this other man's child. I thought you might be, too. But I didn't care. I was the one raising you. You were my daughter.

"A few years ago, your mom started having a rough time again. We'd been doing okay for a while, but she got restless. She saw this thing on TV about a place where you could send away by mail and get a paternity test. She sent my toothbrush and hair from your brush. That's when we found out for sure you were my daughter. The revelation devastated her."

A sob caught in her dad's throat. Carly reached up and squeezed his hand. He cleared his throat and looked down at her with a forced smile.

"She started resenting you then. She already resented me. I think you were starting college at the time. But you are a part of me, and she doesn't like me. You remind her of me. You remind me of myself, too. I like that." He squeezed her hand.

"I love your mom. I've never stopped loving her. I work hard every day to show her how much I love her. It doesn't matter what she does to me. I love her. I will love her till the day I die, and I'd rather be with her than any other woman.

"But it hurts me to see how she treats you. You don't deserve that just because you are my child. I don't want you to resent her or be angry at her, but I don't think you have to tolerate her behavior, either. I felt you needed to know all that."

Carly pulled her knees to her chest and wrapped her arms around her legs. She sat in stunned silence.

"I've always wondered what I did to make her act like this. She changed, almost overnight and I couldn't figure out what I'd done. I guess I didn't do anything."

"No, sadly you are suffering for what I did. I still see a counselor every now and then. He keeps me accountable, helps me keep perspective. It doesn't matter how your mom treats me. I have a responsibility to love her anyway."

Carly shook her head. "I don't know how you do it. It hurts so bad when she acts like that. I want to go…" Carly hesitated. She wanted to say, "…kill myself," but she knew her dad wouldn't understand that. "I want to go hide somewhere. But you deal with it far more than I do. I admire you for sticking with her even when she is awful."

"Ah, it's not that big of a deal. I love her."

He stood and picked up another box. "I'll get these loaded up and then heat some lunch while you finish."

Carly worked, lost in thought. Her dad made it sound easy. Carly knew it couldn't be as simple as he made it sound. Maybe it took practice. Maybe some people had an easier time than others.

She touched the necklace her dad had given her for her birthday. She hadn't taken it off except when she showered. This gift held new special meaning for her. It would be a reminder to her of how her dad chose to love her mom, even when she didn't love him in return. Carly wanted to love her mom like that, too.

She finished packing the last of the things she planned to store in their garage. She and Dad worked to get all the boxes out and into the space he had cleared for them. Then Carly went back to her room and stood in the doorway.

The room was stripped bare, no sheets on the bed, the dresser and desk empty, no pictures on the walls or desk, no curtains on the windows. All trace that she had lived there was gone. Carly's heart clenched in her chest. She felt as though her mom was doing just that—trying to erase all trace that her daughter had lived there.

Dad came up behind her and put his hand on her shoulder. "Looks pretty bare, huh?"

Carly nodded. She didn't trust herself to talk around the lump in her throat.

Dad squeezed her shoulder and turned away. "Come on. I have some of my special hamburgers left from the other day. And baked beans. We even have a couple of slices of cheesecake left that I saved because I knew you were coming."

"That sounds great, Dad." Carly followed her dad up the hall to the kitchen.

Chapter Nineteen

Carly dropped the boxes at Goodwill. Then she drove back to Grandma's house. She'd gotten the name of Dad's counselor. It turned out to be Pastor Conner. She'd met him at Parker and Alice's wedding. Her route to Grandma's took her past First Baptist Church. A car sat in the parking lot. The pastor was locking up the church for the night. Carly pulled into the parking lot on an impulse and parked her car. She got out before she could change her mind.

"Pastor Conner?" she called out as she approached the man.

Pastor Conner looked toward her, a puzzled smile on his face. "Have we met?"

"I was at Parker and Alice's wedding a few weeks ago. We met then. I think you know my father, Richard Warren. I'm Carly."

"Ah! Yes! I remember you."

Carly didn't know what to say next.

"How can I help you?" Pastor Conner stood patiently, a smile fixed on his face.

"I, well, I'm not sure where to start. I know my father meets with you now and then. I was sort of…I mean, I need to talk to someone, and I was wondering if you had time…" Carly let her voice trail off. Her anxiety made it difficult to talk.

"Typically, I don't counsel women. I let my wife do that. She is very good at reading people and getting to the heart of things. She is also a sweet, kind lady."

"Is she available? I mean, does she have time to talk?"

Pastor Conner looked down at his watch. "She's probably home right now if you want to meet her. I imagine you met her at the wedding, too, but there were a lot of people there. and it's easy to get confused."

"Is it far to your house?" Carly asked.

Pastor Conner pointed to a white house with a porch and a gable across the street from the church. "It's there."

Carly looked at the car in the lot, puzzled.

"That belongs to Shondra, our church secretary. She's still in the office."

Carly remembered Shondra. She had played the piano at the wedding. "Okay, if you don't think she'll mind, I'd love to meet your wife."

Carly walked across the street with Pastor Conner. The man chatted about this plant or that flower in his flower beds, pointing them out as they walked along. Carly's nerves eased. Her anxiety disappeared completely when she saw Mrs. Conner.

The bespectacled lady opened the back door for them as they walked up. She wore a bright apron over an old-fashioned looking light blue dress. Her hair was up in a bun. Fuzzy slippers completed the look.

"Welcome!" she said, showing Carly into the little kitchen. Carly received several firm pats on the back. "Carly, isn't it?"

Carly couldn't believe Mrs. Conner remembered her name. "Yes...yes, I'm Carly. Carly Warren."

"I'd heard your Grandma was sick. How's she doing now?" Mrs. Conner asked. She led Carly to the kitchen table and set a full coffee cup on the table in front of her, motioning toward the sugar bowl and non-dairy creamer on the table next to the wall.

Carly looked around for Pastor Conner. He received another cup of coffee and a warm kiss from his wife. With a grin at them both, he disappeared into another part of the house.

Carly added cream and sugar to her coffee. "Grandma is doing better. I live with her to help her keep up with things."

Mrs. Conner sat down in the chair opposite Carly with her own cup of coffee. "What a wonderful opportunity for you. She is such a special lady. We've had her on our prayer list for several weeks now."

Carly relaxed further, a smile spreading across her face. "Yes, she is special. I love her so much. She's patient with people. I thought I would be bored staying with her, that we'd run out of things to talk about or do, but we haven't. She's teaching me how to make quilts."

Carly felt she could talk to Mrs. Conner and she would understand. She shared about the quilt they had finished, how it was meant for her mom and dad, that her mom hadn't wanted it. She'd ended up selling it to someone who did. She shared about the hurt and the pain of rejection she'd felt. She shared all these things without the violent emotion that had been plaguing her for days.

Mrs. Conner listened, nodded now and then, and asked questions, leading Carly on in the narrative. She swiped a tear away and squeezed Carly's hand where it rested on the table. She took Carly to a back bedroom and showed her a blanket she was making for a grandson heading to college in a few weeks—a t-shirt quilt. Carly exclaimed over it, wishing she'd kept some of those old t-shirts from college that she'd donated to goodwill.

They went back into the kitchen, and Carly saw the time on the wall clock—almost five o'clock in the evening.

"Oh!" she exclaimed. "I've got to get back! Uncle Walter will be needing to leave."

"You come by anytime you want, Carly. I enjoyed our visit!" Mrs. Conner wrapped her arms around the younger woman and hugged her.

Carly hugged back. She believed Mrs. Conner. "I will," she promised.

Carly walked back across the road to her car in the church parking lot. The other car was gone. Shondra must have gone home. She got into her hot car and pulled onto the road. The conversation from this morning and this afternoon replayed over and over in her mind.

She'd gone to see Mrs. Conner for counseling. She'd expected an office with a desk and Mrs. Conner jotting notes and asking questions that made Carly reveal her deepest emotions. But even though that hadn't happened, Carly had still talked about all the things that were troubling her, and Mrs. Conner had listened. The emotions that she'd struggled with the last several days were still there, but they no longer threatened to overwhelm her.

Carly felt like crying again, but this time with relief. For the first time in several days, she had hope. She knew she didn't need to wish she were dead. She had a grandma who loved her. A dad who loved her.

And Will.

She didn't know where things were going with him, but he was in her life now, and she was happy about that. She could be happy. She would be happy.

Chapter Twenty

C arly and Grandma started the quilt for Uncle Walter and Aunt Ellen the following day. Grandma patiently gave instructions, and Carly managed to muddle through. She tried to move slowly, deliberately. Dad had always said, "Measure twice, cut once." Carly said that over and over to herself, checking every cut twice before she used the rotary cutter on the fabric. She still made mistakes, but she was getting the hang of it.

"You seem to be feeling better," Grandma commented that afternoon while they were eating lunch.

"I talked to some people yesterday."

"Really? Who?"

"Well, first I spent some time talking with my dad. Sorting through things and getting rid of stuff at their house was…cathartic, I guess. I feel like I have less baggage. I guess I do have less baggage." She laughed at the thought.

"Did you get rid of a lot of stuff?" Grandma asked.

"I took several full boxes to the Goodwill drop-off yesterday. Then I boxed up a lot of photos and other stuff from my childhood and put them in my parent's garage. I guess I'll figure out what to do with it later."

"Good! I always love how much lighter I feel when I get rid of things I don't need."

Carly leaned forward, a new idea coming to mind. "Do you have any sorting and cleaning that you've been ignoring?" she asked. "I can help with it."

Grandma sat back and considered the offer. "I'll have to think about that. We might need to get your mom and aunt involved, which could be tricky. But yes, I do have some things it would be nice to go through." She took another couple of bites, lost in thought. "I'm an old woman. I've spent my whole life accumulating stuff. I've lived in this house for over sixty years. I'm sure I have more than a few things I need to get rid of."

Grandma continued. "Who else did you talk to?"

"I stopped by First Baptist and saw Mrs. Conner. She said to tell you she was thinking of you and praying for you. She said she wanted to get by to see you soon."

"Harriet is such a dear. I've missed her! I'm glad you went to see her. She is such a lovely lady. She has a good word to say about everyone."

"Yes, she is a lovely lady. She had some wonderful things to say about you. She showed me a t-shirt quilt she is making for her grandson. It's an idea to store away for another time, I guess."

"She really helped you, didn't she?" Grandma asked.

"Yes, she did. I didn't even realize she was helping me until I'd left. The last few days have been so dark. I…I've felt like my life wasn't worth living. But after talking with her and Dad, I feel like I have hope, like life is worth living." Carly reached across the table and squeezed Grandma's soft hand. "I get to spend my days with you, Grandma."

"That's why you're all excited about this new project."

"Sort of. But I think Aunt Ellen will like the quilt, even if it doesn't match her bedroom, don't you? Besides, I have a better idea of what I'm doing this time."

She got up from the table and cleared away their dishes. Then they went to the back bedroom to work on their project. The day was warm and stuffy. Grandma dozed off in the chair. It wasn't long before she began to snore.

Carly looked at her Grandma with love. The frail body hid a strong woman, a woman who'd raised children even after her husband died, a woman who'd managed to keep them in school with food on the table for all those years.

Carly didn't feel strong. She remembered a conversation she'd had with Grandma a few years back. Grandma had insisted that she wasn't strong, either. "I relied on the strength of another." Carly had been confused at the time, but it made more sense now.

She thought about her dad and how he was able to love her mom, even when she was unlovable. She'd asked him about that. "I can love her until the day I die because I'm following the example of another who loved me so much, He gave his life for me."

Carly returned her focus to the project in front of her. She needed to concentrate so she wouldn't make silly mistakes. She looked at the instructions for the quilt Grandma had chosen years earlier and found the measurement for the next strip she had to cut. She worked for a while, listening to Grandma snore with her feet up. This cutting part was the most tedious, she decided. Grandma had finished most of it for the last quilt.

She stretched out her back and slipped into the kitchen for a cup of coffee. Her eyes fell on the church calendar from First Baptist hanging on the side of the refrigerator.

Carly knew who'd given Grandma strength and taught Dad how to love. She'd met Him years earlier but had let her life get too busy…He'd been crowded out. Carly thought back to when the whole family had been in church together. Jesus had been a near and dear friend in those days. Then they'd moved and had never found another church. Carly suspected that was because Mom didn't want to go. They'd visited several churches and eventually stopped looking.

Carly thought back to Bible camps and Vacation Bible School. She'd read her Bible faithfully for many years—until near the end of high school when she'd been busy with everything and she didn't think she had time for anything but school and work.

Something Mrs. Conner had said the day before sprang to mind. They'd been talking about Grandma's sweet spirit despite all her health problems. "Sometimes God gives us these things, so we learn to rely on Him when we're weak."

Carly had wondered about that. Why would God give a sweet, caring woman debilitating pain? It seemed cruel. Grandma never complained. Instead, she kept her pleasant, thankful spirit.

It hit Carly. God had given her this struggle with her mom so she would look to Him to learn how to forgive as He forgave Carly and love as He loved Carly.

Carly sank into the kitchen chair. She couldn't do that. What He was asking was too hard.

She touched the necklace at her throat and thought of her father loving her mother for all these years. A tear slid down her cheek. She looked up at the ceiling, imagining she could see straight into heaven.

"I can't do this," Carly whispered. "I can't love her like you love me. I'm not strong like Dad and Grandma."

A quiet voice whispered into her heart, "In your weakness, my strength is made perfect. When you are weak, but you rely on Me, that is when you are strong."

Sobs shook Carly's shoulders as she sat with her head resting on her arms on the table. Relief flooded her heart as the hurt and struggle melted away, replaced with new trust in Someone who would carry her. Someone who loved her and approved of her no matter what she did.

After a while, Carly stood and wiped the tears away. She washed her face at the kitchen sink and then went back to the sewing room, a different woman than she had been when she'd left it a few minutes earlier.

Chapter Twenty-one

The days fell into a pleasant rhythm. Will came three days a week. Carly looked forward to his visits. She also looked forward to seeing him at the running club on Saturdays when he could attend. She and Nadine ran together two mornings a week, and Carly learned to enjoy that time together.

Each week the distances got easier. Nadine kept insisting they run longer. Carly learned to settle into a steady pace and breathe through everything. She registered for the Lincoln Square Clinic 5K, only a few Saturdays away.

The quilt took shape. Carly was pretty sure she liked this one better than the last one. Grandma laughed when Carly confessed this to her. "I thought that every time I made a new one. I even thought I might keep each quilt, even if it was intended as a gift. Just think how many I'd have now if I did that!"

Carly laughed, too, and kept working.

She was happier now. Dark thoughts didn't plague her anymore. She continued to see Mrs. Conner whenever she had a chance.

One morning, Will was writing yet another adjustment to Grandma's medicine on the chart while Carly looked over his shoulder.

"I should make up a new one of those," she muttered.

"You know what is what, right?" asked Will, suddenly concerned.

"Yes. But if someone else had to get her medicine for her, they might not be able to figure it out."

"Ah, yes. I see your point. Well, whatever you want to do." He handed the list back to Carly, and she turned to put it on the fridge.

"You want to come with me to my company picnic?" Will asked.

Carly turned back to him, eyebrows raised. "Is it this evening?"

Will laughed. "I was asking for that. No, It's not until the weekend after the 5K. I thought I'd give you a couple week's warning this time."

"I'd enjoy going with you."

"Great!" Will stood there for a minute, hand on the back of his head, his gaze on his shoes. "I…well, I guess I'm not good at this, but I would love to go out with you before that." He lifted his eyes to meet hers.

"I'd like that, too. I need to stay here with Grandma, though. It'll be hard for me to get away."

Will nodded. "I thought of that. I said I wanted to 'go out' but I should have said 'can we have a date.' There is some great carry out places close by. I thought maybe I could grab something after work and bring it here and we could eat out on the back porch."

A warm sensation flooded Carly's heart. He'd been thinking about her. He'd been planning ways to get to spend time with her, working around her special circumstances. She felt her face flush but not with embarrassment. Carly met Will's gaze and gave him a warm smile.

"I'd like that. Very much. Grandma will give us space if we want it."

"It might be pretty late," Will said, apologetic. "I don't even get off work until after seven most nights. Then I have to finish paperwork, get the food. Well, you get the picture."

Carly shook her head. "Don't worry about that. I still want to do it."

Will relaxed. "I want to, too. I've been wanting to since the wedding, before that even. Will tomorrow night work?"

Carly chuckled. "You sure you don't want to start tonight?"

"Seriously? I thought that might be too soon, but if it works for you, I'd love it!"

Carly turned red all the way up to her hair. "I was teasing you but…"

Will's face fell. "We can wait until tomorrow night."

"No, let's plan for tonight. I was ribbing you about the short notice with the wedding. I'd love it if you came over tonight." Carly reached out and touched his upper arm.

"I know this great Chinese place that has the best carry out. I'll bring that over around eight-ish." Will waved and ran up the walk to his car.

Grandma looked up at Carly as she closed the front door. "He left rather abruptly. Is everything okay?"

Carly couldn't keep the smile off her face. "He's coming back later. After work. He's bringing supper for the two of us."

Grandma laughed with delight and clapped her hands. "Oh, I'm happy for you! Well, dearie, you'll have to get my supper for me early so I can be in my room by then."

"You don't have to go to your room, Grandma. I'm sure he won't mind you being around."

"You might find this hard to believe, Carly, but he isn't coming to see me. He's coming to see you. You don't need an old lady getting in your way."

As promised, Grandma settled in her room early. Carly felt bad, but she didn't seem to mind at all. Her normal bedtime wasn't that far off. She said she'd listen to some of the books on CD that Carly had gotten her from the library.

Carly tried not to fidget as she waited for Will to get there. She didn't change clothes. He was coming straight from work. He would still be in scrubs. She got out two plates and set the table. She filled glasses with ice water. Then she paced in an effort to use up nervous energy. She couldn't sit even if she tried.

When she heard a knock on the front door, Carly almost jumped out of her skin. She took several deep breaths to help bring her heart rate back to normal again. Then she answered the door.

Will stood on the front steps with a plastic bag in one hand and two bottles of Pepsi in the other. "I come bearing food. I hope you're hungry because I think I ordered too much."

Carly waved him into the house. "I have to confess I've been pacing. I'm nervous for some reason. I don't think I can eat. You're over several times a week. I shouldn't be this nervous."

"Yeah, but I wasn't trying to impress you during those visits. I was doing my job." He followed Carly to the kitchen. "I'm nervous, too. That's probably why I ordered too much food."

Carly took the bag and placed each container on the kitchen table. Then she got spoons for each of the containers.

"How was the rest of your day?" she asked as she sat down. She had relaxed as she did all the normal things, like getting the food ready to serve and making sure they had napkins.

"Pretty typical. Busy. I drive a lot. Traffic was terrible tonight. Well, okay, that isn't completely true. It was normal, but I was in kind of a hurry to get back, so it seemed worse than usual."

They dished out their food. The conversation flowed. Time passed without either of them realizing. At a half past ten, Carly looked up at the clock in the kitchen and groaned.

"I have to meet Nadine at six-thirty in the morning. I'm guessing you have to work."

"I have a half day at the hospital and then three visits in the afternoon. Yeah, I have to get going." He made no move to stand up from the table.

Carly glanced down at the table and then up at him. "We have enough food left that you could come for supper tomorrow night, too."

Will's response was subdued but no less eager. "I'd love that. I'll plan for it. Hope your grandma doesn't mind going to bed early two nights in a row."

"I'm sure she won't. She was happy you were coming over. Besides, she has a book she is listening to, and she wanted to finish it. It's long, and I can't imagine she got through the rest of it tonight."

They cleared things up and then she saw him to the door. He hesitated before going outside. His fingers brushed across her chin. His eyes fell to her lips, then came back up to her eyes. One finger came across and touched her lips.

"I'd better go," he breathed, his voice rough with something Carly had never heard there before.

Carly held her breath as Will turned away, walked down the stairs, got into his car, and drove off. She exhaled loudly. Part of her wished he had kissed her, and the other part was thankful he hadn't, not yet. But she couldn't help but wonder, what would it be like to kiss Will?

Chapter Twenty-two

Will came for supper the next evening. He had an all-night shift at the hospital the night following. However, when Carly returned from her run with Nadine the next morning, he was sitting on the front steps with coffee and breakfast sandwiches from a little shop up the road from the hospital. Nadine greeted him before heading inside to clean up for work. Carly joined Will on the steps.

"I know it's already too hot for coffee, but I get to go straight to my other job. I figured I'd better juice up a little," Will explained.

"It's never too hot for coffee," Carly replied, heaving a contented sigh. She took a careful sip of the hot beverage.

"A girl after my own heart. How's the running going? You gonna to be ready for the race?" Will asked between bites.

"Yeah, I'll be ready. Nadine has us running more than five miles now. I don't know how far we went today but something like that. A 5K will seem easy by comparison." Carly took another sip of the coffee. He'd fixed it perfectly. Just the right amount of cream and sugar.

"That's the goal, you know, having the 5K seem easy by comparison. One of these weekends that I have off, I'll have to take you on the park trail. It's a little over six miles of trail through the woods, across wooden bridges, next to moss-covered bluffs. It's beautiful. You would love it." Will looked off in the distance, a dreamy look on his face.

"I don't know. Six miles of trail running. I might need to work up to that. I might need to take it easier after the race. I don't want to push myself too hard and get injured."

"I didn't say we had to run it. We can hike in, have a picnic lunch, and then hike back out. It's entirely up to you." Will turned to her with a smile and handed her a sandwich.

"You got me a sandwich, too! Thanks! I'm starved!"

"We didn't have dinner last night and, unfortunately, I'm going to have to sleep tonight. I thought breakfast together would be fun."

"And me sitting here all sweaty and stinky," Carly said, shaking her head.

"I think you look pretty good." Will reached up and took a strand of hair that had fallen out of her ponytail and tucked it behind her ear.

Carly flushed deep red but didn't move away from his touch.

"Besides, I must be upwind of you. I can't smell a thing."

Carly punched his shoulder and laughed. "Well, with all the time we spend together, I hope you don't get tired of being around me."

"That is *not* possible," Will said. He finished his sandwich, wadded up the wrapper, and stuffed it in the bag. Then he leaned forward and rested his forearms on his knees. "I need to get going, or I'm going to be late. Wish I didn't have to go, though."

Carly wished he didn't have to go, too. She pushed herself to her feet, wincing as her stiff muscles changed position. She hadn't stretched and could feel her muscles complaining with every movement. She waved at Will as he left and then took what was left of her coffee and sandwich inside.

Grandma was shuffling around the kitchen, warming a cup of coffee leftover from the day before when Carly entered.

"You're just getting back?" Grandma asked, looking at the clock.

"Nadine took us on a long run. We didn't get back from that until after seven-thirty and then Will was waiting for me with breakfast." Carly lifted the sandwich to show Grandma.

"I like that boy. He is good to you."

"I like him, too." She felt strange admitting it out loud, but the words filled her with pleasure.

***

The next two weeks until the race passed quickly. Carly made great progress on the quilt. Will came over several nights a week for supper and usually stayed late, even when he needed to be up early the next day. Carly insisted that he didn't have to bring food every time he came. She'd save him a plate from supper and heat it up when he arrived. They talked about everything. A couple of times he brought a movie he insisted she had to see. They'd fix some popcorn and curl up on the couch.

One evening, he wrapped his arm around her shoulders and pulled her next to him. Carly didn't resist. His hand fell to her upper arm. He stroked it absently. She pulled away to shift her position, and he murmured a low complaint.

"Don't move away," he said, reaching for her again.

"My leg is asleep from the knee down."

Will's eyes were intense. He put both arms around her and drew her against his chest. He pulled her legs across his own, almost as though she was sitting in his lap. He rubbed her leg, while Carly twisted her foot around to get the blood flowing again. Carly laid her head on his shoulder.

Will wasn't watching the movie anymore. Carly wasn't either.

"I've never kissed a girl before," Will said. His hand rubbed her arm.

"I've never been kissed," Carly replied.

Will looked at her in disbelief. "I can't believe no guy has ever wanted to kiss you before now."

"I didn't say that," Carly said. "I can't speak for the guys. Some might have wanted to, but I never gave them the chance. What about you?"

"What about me?" Will breathed the words. His face was close to hers.

"Have you ever wanted to kiss a girl before?"

"I don't...I can't think about anything besides how much I want to kiss you right now."

With that, his face dropped the remaining fraction of an inch and his lips touched hers. They lingered there for a moment before he pulled away.

Carly's breath caught. She'd never even imagined his kiss being that enjoyable. His fingers came up and stroked her cheek, her chin. Then he leaned forward and kissed her again.

They were both breathing hard when he pulled away. He rested his forehead against hers, both hands cradling her head and neck.

"That was wonderful," Will whispered, his lips close enough to brush Carly's.

"Yes, it was," Carly agreed.

His hands slid down around her shoulders, and he pulled her against his chest. Carly rested there, content.

Will kissed her again before he left that night, letting his lips linger on hers a moment longer than they had earlier. Carly leaned against the door after he left. The living room felt empty now that Will was gone.

Chapter Twenty-three

The morning of the Lincoln Square Clinic 5K dawned sunny and warm. The weatherman had been forecasting a cold front all week, but it still hadn't arrived. Instead, the day promised to be hot and, even worse, humid.

Grandma and Carly had been talking about the race all week. Grandma wanted to go. She insisted she could cheer Carly on at the beginning and the finish. Carly wasn't sure about that. Will told them there would be tents and chairs where Grandma could sit, but there wouldn't be any relief from the heat. Grandma still insisted she wanted to go.

Will made arrangements with Parker's mom and sister. They would keep an eye on Grandma, and she could help hand out refreshments.

The morning of the race, Carly made breakfast for Grandma and then helped her into the car. Grandma didn't like that Carly hadn't eaten, but she was nervous and sick to her stomach. She was sure she couldn't keep food down if she tried.

They arrived at the clinic parking lot bright and early. The Fire Department was already setting up cooling stations. Large tents provided shade and refreshments for race day registrants. Carly found Parker's mom and helped Grandma to the seat they'd set up for her—a soft camp chair complete with a cup holder containing a bottle of cold water. Grandma could see the starting line from where she was sitting. A look of intense pleasure remained fixed on her face.

Carly attached her race bib and put the timing chip on her shoe. Then she began jogging to warm up and try to work off some of the nerves.

Alice came jogging over and gave Carly a hug. "I'm so glad you decided to come!" she exclaimed.

"Will talked me into it. And Nadine." Carly saw her next-door neighbor jogging from where she'd parked her car several blocks away and waved at her. Nadine joined Carly and Alice on the sidelines.

"Where is Will?" Alice asked.

"He had to work. He was coming straight here. He should be here any time now," Carly said.

As though on cue, Will came jogging toward them. "Ladies," he said with a nod to each of them. "Alice." he nodded toward his sister, a twinkle in his eye.

"Shut up," Alice said and punched his arm.

Will gave her a fake wince and rubbed his arm like her punch had hurt. Then he turned to Carly. "It's your first 5K!"

The sick feeling in Carly's stomach threatened to overwhelm her. She looked around for the nearest port-a-potty or trash can, somewhere to throw up.

Nadine recognized the panic spreading across Carly's face. She reached out and squeezed her shoulder. "You'll be fine. Once you get going, you can channel those nerves and sprint on toward the finish."

Alice nodded agreement. "It's basically flat. You can get a great first race time if you let your nerves work for you. Last year was my first race, and I'm back for more this year."

"I'm glad I'm doing it, but I wish we could get started already and get it over with!"

Parker wandered over with Jasmine in tow. The little girl chattered away, not noticing if anyone was listening or not. Parker stepped close to Alice and planted a firm, lingering kiss right on her mouth.

"Get a room," muttered Will, scowling at his brother-in-law's back.

"You're just jealous," Parker said.

"Nope, pretty sure I'm not jealous. Kind of grossing out over here at a *boy* kissing my *sister* like that." Will made a gagging face.

Parker's expression challenged Will to stop him as he stepped closer to Alice and gave her another kiss, dipping her back in his arms.

Will laughed then. "Okay, okay, you can kiss her all you want *in private*. I'm happy you guys *still* like each other *so* much."

Parker took Jasmine to the tent where Grandma was sitting. His mom was organizing the refreshments for after the race. Grandma called

Jasmine over, and soon she was sitting in Grandma's lap, chattering away, the elderly woman beaming at the child.

Carly looked over at Alice and noticed tears in her eyes.

Alice gave a short, embarrassed laugh. "She starts school Monday. I'm not sure I'm ready for that, but she's about to explode with the excitement of it. Half days, thank God. The house seems empty without her around. I'll get to ease into this gradually."

The master of ceremony's voice came over the loudspeaker. Carly looked around for the first time. Several hundred people were gathered in the road behind the start line.

"Come on!" Nadine grabbed Carly's arm and pulled her toward the start line to claim a spot in the crowd. Carly managed to turn and wave at Grandma and then she followed behind Nadine.

The starting gun sounded, and they were off, the whole group surging forward in tandem, a ripple and murmur of excitement floating over the crowd of runners, while those on the sidelines cheered.

Carly moved forward with Nadine, at first jostling with other runners for position and running space. Little by little space cleared and she could run without having to dodge other runners. She kept pace with Nadine. It felt like a faster pace than they'd used when they practiced but Carly didn't have any trouble with it. The nerves were indeed helping. Nadine went a little faster and passed between two runners. Carly went with her.

Carly strained to see if she could catch sight of Will, Alice, or Parker. They must have been ahead in the crowd at the start line. She stopped looking and focused on running. The miles passed. Carly's legs hurt at the beginning like they usually did when she first started out, but she pushed through the pain.

She caught sight of the finish in the distance. She started to push forward faster.

"Pace yourself," Nadine instructed. "It's still a half mile away. You don't want to lose too much steam before you get there." But she increased her speed as well.

The two women crossed the finish line together.

Grandma and Will were standing on the sidelines. She gripped his arm harder and cheered when she saw Carly cross the finish line. Carly grinned at both of them and ran in their direction as soon as the chip had been removed from her shoe.

They settled Grandma back in her chair and then Carly found water and an apple. Parker and Alice finished the race behind Carly. Nadine's husband, Charles, had been among the first finishers, and he and Nadine came over to chat. They were all making so much noise that Carly almost didn't hear her cell phone ringing. She found her bag and fished out the phone.

Jessie was on the other end.

"Carly," Jessie's worried voice came over the phone, "your dad is in the hospital."

Chapter Twenty-four

"Do you want me to come with you?" Will was folding the camp chair while Carly helped Grandma toward the car. He stopped in front of the two women and put his hand on Carly's shoulder. "I want to help."

Carly forced herself to focus on his face. "I don't know. Someone needs to be with Grandma."

"Jasmine and I can stay with your Grandma." Alice's voice came from behind them. "We only live a couple of blocks away from her according to Will. We'll follow you there now and stay until you can get home."

Grandma smiled at Carly and patted her arm. "I'd sure enjoy having that little one come over to play for a while. Don't you worry about me. I'll be fine."

Carly looked around at Alice. "Thank you. I appreciate you doing this."

"Then I'll come with you to the hospital," Will said.

"Okay, that sounds good." Carly was relieved she didn't have to go alone.

Will and Alice followed Carly to Grandma's house. They got everyone into the house and situated. Carly rinsed off in the shower and put on fresh, non-athletic, clothing. Then they left for the hospital. Will drove. Carly rode in silence, terrified of what she would find at the hospital.

"Did they know what was wrong?" Will asked.

"No. Jessie called as soon as Dale left for the hospital with Dad. They were still en route in the ambulance."

"What about your mom?"

"I don't know."

The silence grew longer, both lost in thought. Finally, Carly spoke again.

"I haven't told any of them we're dating. I just haven't had the chance. Uncle Walter and Aunt Ellen know, but not the rest of the family."

Will smiled over at her. "Don't worry about it." Then he chuckled. "I guess they'll find out today, won't they?"

Carly sagged back into the car seat. "Yes, they will. I'm glad about that."

Will reached for her hand and squeezed it. He rested the back of his hand on her leg. "I can't promise your dad will be okay. I hope he will, but we don't know. I'll be there for you all the way, every time you need me."

Carly felt sick, whether from worry or hunger she couldn't tell. Between her nerves about the race and the news about her dad, she'd barely eaten today.

She squeezed Will's hand in return. Words weren't necessary. He understood.

They arrived at the emergency room entrance, and Will dropped Carly off while he parked the car in the garage across the street.

Carly hurried inside and looked around for Dale, hoping her mom was there too. He sat in the corner leafing through a magazine but not appearing to read any of the words. He looked up as Carly approached.

"I'm glad you're here," he said, wrapping Carly in a bear hug.

"Any news?" Carly asked as she sank into an uncomfortable metal and vinyl chair. For a room where people spend hours waiting and worrying, they didn't go out of their way to make it comfortable, Carly thought. She adjusted how she was sitting, so the metal bar in the seat didn't dig into her leg.

"They're running tests. I was in the room with him but thought I'd better wait out here for you. Jessie said you were on the way. I'll go back in a minute. The orderly said he'd come get me when they finished the CAT scan."

"I'd have been here sooner, but you caught me right as I was finishing a 5K over by Grandma's house."

"I didn't know you were running," Dale said. He looked Carly over. "You look good, best I've seen you in a long time."

Carly rolled her eyes. "Thanks, I guess."

"You know what I mean."

"No, I don't. What do you mean 'I look better than I have in a while'?" Carly folded her arms and leaned back against the chair to wait for his answer.

Dale observed his sister for a moment before answering. "You've always stayed in pretty good shape physically. I guess you look happier, more at peace. Well, as much as you can, given the present circumstances." He waved his hand around indicating their surroundings.

Will walked into the waiting room and headed toward them. He still wore his race number pinned to his running shirt.

"Hey, you didn't eat anything yet today, did you?" he asked Carly as he walked up and sat down next to her.

Carly shook her head. "I had an apple after the race, but I don't know if I can eat anything else right now."

"Well, you should. I'll at least get you some coffee. Probably grab a sandwich for you, too." He leaned around Carly. "Do you need something to eat or drink? There is a great coffee shop up the road. I can get you something while I'm there. I'm Will, by the way." He reached a hand out toward Dale.

"Dale, Carly's older brother. Pleased to meet you." He shook hands with Will. "I'll take some coffee if you don't mind. But I'd already eaten breakfast when we got the call."

"Who called you?" Carly asked Dale.

Will leaned and kissed her cheek. "I'll be back in a few minutes."

"And who is that?" Dale pointed at Will's retreating back.

"That's Will."

Now it was Dale's turn to roll his eyes. "Yeah, he said that."

"Don't interrupt." Carly shook a finger at Dale. "Will and I have been dating for a couple of months now."

"You planned to tell the family...when?"

"I wasn't keeping it from the family. Uncle Walter and Aunt Ellen know about him. Look, we'd only been out once before July fourth, and I haven't seen the rest of the family, aside from Uncle Walter, since then."

"He kissed you."

"Kissing happens. Who died and made you the boss of me?" Carly stopped cold at those words. "I...I'm sorry. I didn't mean...It isn't funny to joke about death with Dad sick."

Dale bumped her shoulder with his own. "I'm your big brother. It's my job to look out for you."

"You don't get any say in this. I'm thirty-six years old."

"Yeah, well, I'm a guy, and guys can tell things about other guys. But I promise to be nice to him. The brief thirty seconds we spent together in male bonding gave me the impression that he takes good care of you."

The orderly walked into the room, and both Dale and Carly stood up.

"He's back in the room. You can come and sit with him if you want. We'll have to take him for another test in a few minutes, but the doctor wants the results from this test first."

"I'll go on back. You wait here for Will," Dale instructed, turning to Carly.

"I want to see Dad. Will works here. I'll send him a text when I see where we are, and he can come back."

Dale shrugged and started toward Dad's room. Carly followed.

Dad was groggy and incoherent when they arrived in the triage room. Carly went to his side and took his hand in her own, giving it a gentle squeeze. He looked at her, his eyes struggling to focus on her face. He mumbled something, and his eyes slid shut.

Carly looked him over. Blood was caked in his hair on the side of his head, and she couldn't see a gash or anything that would have caused it.

"What happened?" Carly asked Dale.

"They don't know yet. The EMTs found him lying on the living room floor, unconscious. The front door was open, and there was a note with my number laying beside him on the floor. The EMT called me. I tried to call Mom but never got through to her."

"I tried to call her, too. It's going straight to voicemail."

"They think he hit his head hard on something and managed to call 911 before losing consciousness. They don't know if the head injury is causing his current symptoms or if something else caused him to fall and hit his head—like a stroke or a seizure. I guess we'll have to keep waiting to find out. Jessie took me to their house, and I rode with him to the hospital."

They sat in silence. Machines beeped. Messages came over the intercom system of the hospital. Nurses and doctors talked and laughed in the hall. Dale and Carly waited and watched.

Carly looked at her dad. He'd always been the strong one, the one who could pick her up and toss her into the air until she was old enough to remember it, the one who gave horseback rides through the house, who built their first tree house and went hunting every fall. It hurt to see him lying weak and helpless in the hospital bed.

Carly fingered the necklace he'd given her for her birthday. She begged God to let her daddy be okay.

"Where is Mom?" Dale growled in frustration. "I can never get ahold of her on Saturdays. She must have turned her phone completely off."

Carly remembered when she was still living at home that Mom would be gone all day Saturday at least once a month. She claimed she was attending an art class. Dad had told her that Mom had been gone every Saturday since she'd moved in with Grandma. Carly thought back to everything her dad had told her and wondered if the 'art class' wasn't a cover for something…else.

Will's arrival interrupted her dark thoughts. He held a coffee holder with three cups in one hand and a bag in the other.

"I didn't know how you like your coffee," he said to Dale, handing him one of the cups. "I got it black. You can go to the nurses' break room for cream and sugar if you want it. I'll show you where it is."

"Nah, I like it black," Dale said, taking a sip of the brew.

"Yours has cream and sugar, just how you like it." Will handed Carly her cup. "I also got you a ham and cheese sandwich. You haven't had one of those yet, and the sauce is worth every bite. I thought it might tempt you to eat, even though you don't feel like it."

Just how you like it? mouthed Dale.

Carly glared at him, then gave Will a grateful smile. "Thanks." She released her dad's hand and took the coffee and sandwich.

"Any news?" Will asked once everyone was settled.

"Not yet. The doctor hasn't been around to check on things," Dale said.

Will stood and stepped outside the door to look at the chart, then came back. "I know the doctor. He can be a little…slow…on his emergency room shift. If he hasn't been around once I finish this sandwich, I'll go see if I can shake things loose for you."

"What floor did you work last night?" Carly asked.

"Emergency room, ironically. It's slow this morning. Kind of unusual for a Saturday. You shouldn't have to wait this long."

"You worked all night last night?" Dale asked. He looked surprised at the news.

"Will works part-time at the hospital as a nurse. He went straight to the race from his shift last night and then brought me here when Jessie called," Carly explained.

"Wow. Thanks, man. I really appreciate that."

"It's nothing. If I get desperate, I can go take a nap in the break room. Besides, I'm off the rest of today and all day tomorrow."

"Will is Grandma's home care nurse. That's how we met."

"You work a full-time job and a part-time job and still have time to date my sister."

"You told him?" Will looked at Carly, eyebrows raised.

Carly nodded. "He took the news pretty well, considering he threatened to kill anyone I dated in high school and college. No attempts on your life just yet."

Will turned back to Dale. "I'm hyperactive. I have to stay busy, or I get bored and into trouble." He grinned.

Dale didn't find it amusing. He folded his arms across his chest and narrowed his eyes. "What kind of trouble?"

Will put both hands up. "Nothing serious. Extreme sports, LAN parties, weekend-long battle strategy games, that kind of thing."

Dale's face broke into a huge grin. "LAN parties! I'll have to introduce you to a couple of my friends. We can plan a get-together." Then his face fell. "I'll have to talk to my wife about it first, though. She doesn't like it when I spend the weekend doing that."

Carly couldn't help but laugh. "Jessie won't let you, eh? Who is the boss of *you*?"

"I think it's nice that he considers his wife's feelings." Will's face was serious, but his eyes twinkled at Carly.

"You two be careful. One of these days you'll figure out that it really matters what the other person in the relationship thinks and how they feel."

Carly's face softened. She thought about Dad enduring years of a marriage where one partner did whatever they wanted without regard for the other. She looked up at Dale.

"Jessie would probably let you have a weekend LAN game once in a while."

"Yeah, she will. She doesn't mind too much. Nate is getting old enough to play, too."

"Nate?" asked Will.

"You need to meet the whole family. Nate is Dale's oldest son. He's twelve," she said.

"Ah," said Will as he crumpled up his sandwich wrapper and threw it in the trash. "Well, time's up. I'm going to go find that doctor and see if we can get things moving around here."

"I like him," said Dale. "I'm not saying that because I have to, either. He's got a lot going for him."

Carly flushed. "I'm glad you like him. You think Dad and Mom will like him?"

"Dad will. I can guarantee that. I don't know about Mom. She's been acting so strange lately. I wish I knew what was going on there."

Carly looked up at him, puzzled. "How do you mean, strange?"

"Well, Independence Day she went off on you. A couple of weeks ago, Jessie dropped by with the kids after a trip to the library, and she went off on Jessie. Jessie said she looked like she'd just gotten out of the shower, even though it was in the afternoon. She got all over her for not calling before they came, even though she's told Jessie she wants them to feel like they can drop by anytime. Then, when the kids went into the toy room to play, she got after them for wrecking it. Jessie didn't stay. She packed everyone up and left and told the kids Grandma must not be feeling well, which was why she wasn't dressed yet.

"Now, we've been trying to reach her and can't get through. This isn't the first time she's done this. I had to get Dad to help me fix the lawn mower last weekend. Mom wasn't there, and he said she was gone most weekends."

Carly observed her dad where he lay unconscious in his hospital bed. Why did he tolerate her mom acting that way? Carly felt like he was enabling her bad behavior. But maybe she really *did* have an art class on Saturdays. And maybe her mom was lazy during the week and stayed in her PJs all day. Carly didn't want to contemplate the other possibility, the one that had been niggling at the back of her mind ever since she'd gotten to the hospital.

"I don't know, Dale. I do know Dad loves her a great deal. If he's willing to tolerate some things, maybe we should be, too."

"Tolerate some things?" Dale asked. "What do you know that I don't?"

Carly's gut clenched. She shouldn't have said anything. Or maybe her brother was smart enough to put things together for himself. She opened her mouth to answer his question when they heard voices in the hall. The next moment, Will and the doctor pushed the door open and entered the room.

Chapter Twenty-five

A few inconclusive tests later, Dad was moved to a hospital room. Will didn't rest all morning, working as their advocate to help move things along so Dad could receive the proper care. The CT scan showed nothing except the symptoms of a concussion. An x-ray showed the same thing.

"He needs a neurologist to look at him," the doctor told them late in the morning. "I'll arrange for him to have someone look in on him, once he is in a real room."

Richard was admitted to the hospital, still semi-conscious. Dale said he'd stay for a while longer, even spend the night if needed. Jessie could come and relieve him the next morning. Carly needed to get back to Grandma, and Will needed sleep.

It was mid-afternoon when Will drove Carly home. Carly felt both physically and emotionally worn down. She could only imagine Will's exhaustion. She tried calling her mom. Again, it went straight to her voicemail.

"What should I do if I suspect someone I love of doing something horrible to another person I love?" she asked Will.

Will looked puzzled. "I might need a bit more context than that."

"I don't know how much I should tell you." Carly looked out her window, trying to decide if she should confide in him or not. She hadn't told anyone about her conversation with Dad, not even Grandma.

"Now I'm curious," Will said, glancing over at Carly.

Carly turned her body to face him. "I'm going to tell you something that I haven't told anyone, not even Grandma. I have to share this with someone. I can't carry it alone anymore.

"Years ago, my mom had an affair with a man that lasted for several years. She even thought I might be this other man's daughter. She almost left my dad for him. I think she might be having another affair right now."

Will let out a low whistle. "That's a load to bear. When did you find out about this?"

"Around Independence Day. My dad told me so I'd be better able to understand my mom's behavior. I don't know why he hasn't left her yet. She barely tolerates having him around, but when you watch him with her, he treats her with love and respect."

"I can't wait to meet your dad. He sounds like a remarkable man."

"He is." Carly's voice was soft.

"Why did you need to tell me about it?"

"I can't keep carrying this burden alone," Carly said around the lump in her throat. "I think I have to confront Mom about it."

Will's expression was full of compassion. "I won't be much more than moral support."

"I'd rather have your moral support than anyone else's. I don't want to say anything to Dale until I have more information.

"You have to be exhausted." Carly reached out and brushed her fingers down his jawline.

Will caught her hand and kissed her fingertips. "I am pretty tired. But I'm glad I could be there to help you today. It's worth being tired."

Alice and Jasmine were still at Grandma's house when they arrived home. Uncle Walter had been by earlier in the afternoon but had left right away to go to the hospital to see Carly's dad.

Jasmine was busy with a needle and thread that Grandma had gotten out for her. She'd jabbed the thread through randomly a few times, then, seeming to get the hang of it, she started working on making a picture with the thread. Alice relaxed on the couch watching the little girl. Grandma fairly bubbled with excitement and the pleasure of having a child in the house.

Will and Carly filled them in on what had happened at the hospital, then Alice left for home, promising to come again.

Will left soon afterward, but not before taking Carly into his arms and holding her against his chest. She clung to him. He held her until she pulled back and looked up at him. He brushed a stray tear away with his thumb.

"Call me as soon as you get any news at all, good or bad," he said and brushed a kiss across her lips. Then he left, too.

Carly went back into the house, drained and exhausted from the day. "You want to use some of our fun money and eat out?" she asked Grandma as she came in and sank onto the couch.

"We don't need to do anything too fancy. We should try that Chinese place Will likes," Grandma said.

"They only do carry out, but if you don't mind, I'll drive over and pick it up, and then we can eat it here and head to bed early."

Grandma sighed. "That sounds nice. It's been a long day. A good day, but a long day."

"I'm not sure if it's all been good," Carly said with a small sigh of her own.

"Oh, I'm sorry dearie. That isn't what I meant. I was thinking about the race and little Jasmine being here. I know it's been hard for you. Thank God Will was there for you!"

Yes, thank God for Will, thought Carly. Even Dale had been relying on him. She pushed herself up from the couch, went to the kitchen, and got the phone number for the Chinese restaurant. When she picked up her phone, she saw that Will had sent her a text message.

Wish I didn't have to leave you. Praying for you and your dad.

Chapter Twenty-six

Carly wasn't able to reach her mom on the phone the next day. Dale couldn't either. He called Carly, almost beside himself with concern. He'd gone by the house that morning, and her car wasn't in the driveway.

Carly hoped her mom had gotten their voice messages and would come to the hospital, but when she and Grandma arrived mid-morning, she found Dad alone in his room.

He'd improved somewhat in the night. He was conscious and could talk, but his eyes wouldn't focus, and his words were incoherent. He smiled when they came into the room. Grandma sat down in the chair. She spoke to him in a low voice, and he mumbled something back. Carly stood to the side and listened.

"You all won't be able to stay long," a nurse said, entering the room. "Mr. Warren needs a lot of sleep right now."

"We won't be here long," Carly assured her. "Has the doctor been in this morning?"

"The shift doctor was here earlier. Your dad's doctor should be here anytime. He said he was going to stop in before lunch."

Dad fell asleep. So did Grandma. Carly pulled out the book she'd brought to read and settled in to wait. She'd almost decided to leave when the doctor arrived.

He checked her dad and looked at his charts. Then he looked up at Carly. "Legally, I'm not allowed to talk with you about this. The only person I'm allowed to give information to is your father's stated next of kin, which is your mother."

Carly shook her head. "I don't even know if my mom knows my dad is here. My brother and I have been trying to reach her on the phone since yesterday morning and haven't been able to."

The doctor looked at the charts again, then back up at her. "Given the circumstances, and because of his condition, I'm going to treat you and your brother like next of kin. Based on the tests we did last night and the MRI he had this morning, the neurologist and I think he had a seizure, which caused him to lose consciousness, fall, and hit his head, causing a severe concussion. It's nothing short of miraculous that he was able to maintain enough mental clarity to write down your brother's number and dial 911. We can't release him from the hospital until the worst of the symptoms subside, and we are confident the bleed on his brain isn't getting worse. Right now, he needs to rest and heal. Should there be any change, where can I reach either you or your brother?"

Carly gave the doctor the information he needed.

"It would be a good idea for you to find a way to reach your mom. At this point, he could get worse without any warning. Usually, the first three to four hours are the most critical, after that, the first twenty-four. But with the severity of his injury and the fact that we aren't certain what caused it, it would be best to be prepared."

Carly and Grandma left for home not long after the doctor's visit. Dad was sleeping so she didn't see any reason to stay. She called Dale on the way and told him what the doctor had said.

"I've been trying to reach Mom. Jessie has, too," Dale said. "I'm starting to worry about her. It's been more than twenty-four hours. Do you think we need to call the police?"

"I don't know, but I'm concerned too. Let me stop by the house and see what I can find. Maybe she went somewhere for the weekend and left numbers where we could reach her."

"But she didn't take her cell phone?" Dale sounded annoyed.

"Again, I don't know. I'll have to go see what I can figure out at their house. I'm on my way there now."

Carly hung up and turned to Grandma. "Change of plans. We're going to see what we can find out about Mom and why we haven't been able to reach her."

"You do what you need to do, Carly. I'm not tired yet."

Carly used her key to open her parent's house. She found a mess in the living room. Latex gloves, empty gauze packages, and packages from the IV they'd started in the living room lay strewn around. Bloody gauze lay off to one side. Carly could see a bloody handprint where Dad had pushed himself up on the edge of an end table to reach the phone. Carly saw another one on the wall by the door from the dining room. She went that direction. She found another bloody smear where he'd grabbed the back of a dining room chair and still another on the door jamb leading to the garage. The garage door stood open, flooding the kitchen and dining room with hot air from the garage.

Carly stepped into the garage and looked around. Dad's table saw had been set up on his workbench and a long piece of wood still stuck out from it, clamped down. Dad's safety glasses lay on the floor next to a small, dried pool of blood. Bloody handprints marked a path from the blood pool to the door. Dad must have crawled his way over to the wall, too incoherent and off balance to stand any sooner.

Carly felt sick. He could have killed or maimed himself on one of his power tools if the accident had happened a moment sooner or later. Her mom would have come home to a dead husband. Carly winced as she thought of that gruesome scene. She leaned against the door jamb to steady herself and draw her focus back to the job at hand.

She could come clean it another day. She needed to find her mom. Closing the door to the garage behind her, she went into the kitchen to look at the calendar Mom kept on the side of the refrigerator. Nothing was marked on it except a note on Saturday that said *Art class, eight a.m., M's.*

Carly thought for a while. "M" had to be the initial of whoever was hosting the craft class that week. Carly looked down the list of phone numbers also posted on the side of the fridge to see if any began with that letter. The name "Marlene" caught her attention. Carly grabbed the phone and called the number. A woman answered the phone.

"Hello? Is this Marlene?" Carly asked

"Yes. Who is this?"

"I'm Susan Warren's daughter, Carly. Mom marked on the calendar that she was going to be at your house for art class yesterday. The thing is, we've had a family emergency, and we can't reach her on the phone."

The woman's voice softened. "I'm sorry. I can't help you. Susan hasn't been to the craft class in months. She only came once or twice, anyway. And we changed it to Thursday night instead of Saturday morning."

"Ah." Carly leaned against the counter, not sure where to go from here. "Thank you for your time. Sorry to have bothered you."

"Not a problem. Wish I could help you more. I hope you find your mom."

Carly disconnected the call and stared at the receiver in her hand for a long time. She considered her next step and decided to check her parent's room to see if her mom's clothing was still there.

The room hadn't been repainted yet. The old curtains and bedspread were still in place. Carly walked through the room to the dresser and opened the drawers. All the clothing was still inside.

Carly felt like a thief as she rifled through her mom's drawers, looking for anything that would tell them where she'd gone. The back of the bottom drawer felt odd to her. She managed to work her hand along the top and back of it. A piece of cardboard had been cut to fit the back of the drawer. When Carly shifted it around, it slid out, and several photos fell forward.

Her mom and another man stood beaming in a dozen different photos. The back of one said, *Here's to the best of times, Mark.* Ah, that would be the "M" on the calendar. The pictures showed the two snuggled together on a couch at a party, perched on bar stools with their cheeks together, and kissing under some mistletoe in winter clothing. In all of them, her mom looked happy. Not the fake happy that she put on when company came over or when she was trying to be perky to "help Carly feel better".

Angry waves flooded through Carly. She discovered she was clenching her jaw and one fist. Spots appeared before her eyes as waves of the rage and betrayal washed over her. Carly stood and gripped the edge of the dresser for support. The pictures lay discarded on the floor. That's when she noticed the cell phone sitting on top of the dresser. The cell phone she'd been trying to call for almost two days.

Carly heard the garage door begin to open, and gasped. Her mom must not know she'd been discovered. She replaced everything in the back of the drawer just as it had been before she disturbed it. She put the contents of the drawer in order and checked each of the others to make sure they looked like they should. Then she made her way to the living room, hoping to get there before her mom entered the house.

Carly and her mom walked into the living room at the same time. "Mom? Carly? What are you doing here? What's all this mess?" she asked, looking around in shock. "Why is there blood in the garage?"

Carly bit back the angry response on the tip of her tongue. "Dad's had an accident. He's in the hospital. They don't know yet what caused it. They think it might have been a seizure, but he hit his head on something and has a bad concussion. He'll be in there for at least a couple more days, maybe even a week."

"Oh, that's terrible!" Mom exclaimed. She looked around at the mess in the living room. "You left all this for me to clean up?"

Carly swallowed hard. Her dad was in the hospital, and all her mom could think about was the stupid mess in the living room.

"I haven't had a chance to clean it yet. We've been trying to reach you on the phone since yesterday. Why didn't you answer your cell phone?"

"I think I left it here. I can't find my cell phone anywhere. It isn't in my purse. Maybe the battery died. I don't know." Susan pointed to the mess on the floor. "I'll get you some rags, and you can get started."

Grandma stood from the easy chair where she'd had her feet up. "Carly has to take me home now. We've been gone long enough, and I'm hungry and tired. You'll have to clean this mess. But the mess will wait. Your husband is lying in a hospital bed, and they don't even know what is wrong with him. Your place is there with him."

"It won't do any good to go to the hospital now. Visiting hours are almost over. I'll go see him tomorrow." Susan turned on her heel and left the room.

Carly helped Grandma to the door and down the front steps.

Her mom followed them. "Found the phone! It was on my dresser. But I've got it on now. Call me if you hear or need anything!" She went into the house and shut the door.

"I feel sick," Grandma murmured to Carly. Carly settled her in the car and then went around to the driver's side. Grandma's eyes were closed, her skin pale and gray.

"Grandma, are you alright?" she asked, gripping the old lady's arm. Her pulse was strong and steady.

"I'm fine," Grandma murmured again. "I don't feel all that well. I'm probably hungry. We need to get home. I need to eat."

"Of course," said Carly, backing out of the driveway and heading for home.

Carly pushed the speed limit the whole way there. They were almost home when a sound somewhat like a sob came from the other side of the car. Carly pulled the car over to the side of the road and put it in park. Then she turned her full attention to her grandma.

Tears streamed down the old lady's face. "Something is wrong with my daughter. What happened to her? Why didn't she want to go see her husband? What is wrong with her?"

She gripped the tissue she'd dug out of her purse and made a futile attempt to blow her nose and wipe her eyes.

Tears came to Carly's eyes as well, tears of anger and betrayal and hurt. Tears that made it impossible for her to continue driving home.

They sat in the car and cried together, Grandma because she didn't know what was wrong, and Carly because she did, but didn't know what to do about it.

Chapter Twenty-seven

B oth women were subdued the following morning when Will arrived to check Grandma. Will was on the clock and couldn't linger to visit, but he came and found Carly where she sat on the back patio steps and asked her what had happened. She shared the events of the previous afternoon, taking as little of his time as possible. The anger she'd felt the day before simmered under the surface and her voice shook.

Will laid his hand on her forearm. "I'm worried about you the most, Carly. You're carrying all this alone."

"I don't have a lot of choices, you know?"

"I have to go, or I'll be late for my next visit. It's clear across town. But if you can talk to someone about all this, it would be good." He squeezed her arm again and stood.

Carly stood, too. The next moment, his long arms were encircling her. He nestled her close to his chest. Carly wrapped her arms around him and stood there, his touch soothing her, helping the anger and hurt fade, assuring her everything would be fine.

Will stepped back. Carly was able to smile up at him, a smile that reached her eyes and let him know she would be fine.

"Can I come see you tonight?" he asked, reaching up and brushing a lock of hair out of her face, his fingertips brushing her cheek. "I'll bring dinner."

"I'd love that," Carly almost whispered.

Will released her, trotted down the steps, and disappeared around the side of the house.

Carly looked across the backyard that hadn't been mowed in over a week. She wouldn't have time to do it today. She still needed to get up to the hospital to see her dad.

The phone rang inside the house. With a sigh, Carly turned and went back into the house.

Jessie was on the phone. "Can I come over today and stay with Grandma so you can get up to see your dad?"

Carly hesitated. "It's a long drive, and you're busy with the kids," she finally replied.

"Dale thought Grandma might enjoy having a visit. Besides, it's only Olivia. The other three started school today."

"Oh, that's right. Alice said Jasmine was starting today, too. I should have remembered," Carly exclaimed, hand to her forehead.

"What? Who's Alice?"

"Alice is Will's sister." Carly realized too late that any explanation would be insufficient. "Dale met Will on Saturday."

"Ah, yes. He told me about that. Okay, we'll be by after lunch. Will that work for you?"

"That would be great. I can get up there to see Dad and be back so you can get home before traffic gets bad. See you then!"

Grandma was excited to hear they were coming and relieved that she didn't have to make another trip to the hospital. "I'll see him again in a few days," she said. "But it tires him out, and it tires me out. It isn't helpful for either of us."

Carly was ready to leave as soon as Jessie arrived. She reached the hospital not long after the doctor had made his rounds. The nurse on duty went to get the doctor as soon as she arrived.

Carly sat down by her dad's bed and watched him sleep for a few minutes. He stirred. His eyelids fluttered, then he was still.

The doctor pushed open the door and beckoned Carly out into the hall.

"As you can see, we still have him sedated. The goal is to help his brain heal by letting him sleep as much as he can. If he were awake, he'd be in acute pain. This is better for him overall," the doctor explained.

"Has he been awake at all?" Carly asked.

"We did another MRI this morning to check on the brain bleed. He was awake but didn't say much. He is still confused about where he is or what is going on. The brain bleed hasn't gotten worse, which is good news. We should begin to see it go down in the next couple days, though we still have to monitor the pressure inside his skull."

Carly nodded. "I understand."

"He needs to have his family come visit him, but those visits need to be short," the doctor continued. "Have you managed to get in touch with your mom?"

"Yes, I saw her yesterday and explained what was going on. I was hoping she'd been to see him today. She said she was coming."

The doctor shook his head. "To my knowledge, you are the first person to visit him today, though his son did spend the night with him again."

Poor Dale! Carly thought. *He must be exhausted!*

"I'll try to get in touch with her again today," Carly said.

"Good," said the doctor. "We'll need her signature to do any invasive procedures. Alright, that seems to be everything." He handed Carly a business card with his name and number. "If you have any questions or concerns, please don't hesitate to call me. The first number is my office. The second is the exchange which can be reached any time of the day or night."

"Thank you," said Carly, taking the card from the doctor.

She returned to her dad's bedside and sat next to him again, using the relative quiet of his room to think about what she should do next.

Will was right. She couldn't bear the whole burden alone. But she didn't know who to turn to for advice. Grandma didn't need the extra worry. She didn't know Nadine well enough to talk to her about it. Alice was kindhearted. Carly knew she would listen, but she was busy, too.

Mrs. Conner. Carly hadn't been to see the pastor's wife in over a week. She always enjoyed the visits. Besides, Carly almost had the next quilt finished, and she'd promised to show Mrs. Conner before she gave it to Uncle Walter and Aunt Ellen.

But how would she tell Mrs. Conner about it without seeming like she was trying to make her mom look bad? Besides, was this really any of her business? Carly looked at her father lying in the bed asleep. He didn't know about Mom. He couldn't. Would he allow it to go on if he knew about it? At what point did it stop being about him loving his wife and start being about him enabling her?

Carly fingered the necklace at her throat. She admired her dad. How could her mom miss how great he was and sneak around with another man?

"I love you, Daddy," Carly whispered. She reached out, took her dad's hand in her own, and laid it against her cheek. "I want to be like you when I grow up."

As Carly left the room a few minutes later, she felt like a burden had been lifted from her shoulders. She knew what to do. She felt she could lay everything aside for now and rest.

She walked to her car in the parking garage and sent Will a text. *Don't bring dinner tonight. I'm cooking.* Then she started for Grandma's house, imagining what she would fix for them to eat.

Chapter Twenty-eight

Will brought a movie for them to watch that evening, a comedy that Carly had never seen. They laughed until their sides hurt. Carly loved how Will would belly laugh at a movie he'd seen twenty times. When the movie was over, Will became serious. "You okay?" he asked. "I mean, really okay, not just putting on an act."

Carly relaxed against him. "Yeah. I'm okay. I'm going to try to visit with Mrs. Conner and ask her advice. I got to sit with my dad for a little while today. The doctor said he wasn't worse, even if he wasn't better yet. So, yeah, I'm okay. How 'bout you?"

Will leaned back onto the couch and smiled. "I'm okay, too. I've been worried about you the past couple days. I could hardly think about anything else. I'm better knowing you're better."

Carly snuggled into his side. "Thanks for caring this much. It means a lot to me."

Will couldn't stay too late that night since he had a seven-a.m. shift at the hospital. He told Carly he'd look in on her dad in the morning. Carly watched him from the front steps as he drove up the street. Part way up, he stopped, put the car in reverse and backed down to the house again.

"Don't forget the picnic on Saturday," he called through the open car window.

Carly clapped a hand to her forehead. "I'd forgotten! Too many things happened this weekend. Thanks for reminding me!"

The following morning, Uncle Walter stopped by the house to deal with the lawn. Carly apologized for not taking care of it, but Uncle Walter wouldn't hear it. "You have too many things to think about. Don't make the yard one of them right now."

Carly used the time he was with Grandma to make a trip to the hospital to visit her dad. He hadn't changed much. The doctor said they'd be weaning him off the sedative starting the following day, provided the brain bleed continued to improve. And her mom still hadn't bothered to visit.

Carly thought about going straight back to Grandma's, but she knew she'd have a hard time getting away again later in the day. She detoured to the little white house across the street from First Baptist Church.

Mrs. Conner still had curlers in her hair and was wearing her apron and big fluffy slippers, but she welcomed Carly into the house like nothing was out of the ordinary.

The two women sat at the kitchen table with glasses of iced tea. Carly shared about her dad being in the hospital. Mrs. Conner told her Dale had called Pastor Conner to let him know about the situation. Pastor Conner was going to visit that afternoon.

Carly rolled her eyes. "Everyone is going to visit my dad. Even my boyfriend visited him, and they've never met. But my mom refuses to go see him."

Mrs. Conner sat still, staring into her iced tea. Then she lifted her eyes to meet Carly's. "You probably wonder why your dad tolerates her acting like that."

"You know about it?" Carly was shocked.

"Just the little that my husband shared with me when he needed a woman's perspective."

"I do wonder why he tolerates her. I know he loves her, but I don't understand why he lets her get away with mistreating him."

"He isn't letting her get away with anything. He is allowing himself to be mistreated to show his wife how much he loves her," Mrs. Conner explained.

"He's enabling her."

"He's allowing her to be her own person, not trying to change her to be what he wants her to be."

Carly frowned. "I don't see that. Dad sits around and lets her get away with anything."

"Your dad knows what she's done. There will be consequences for her actions. When that happens, she'll need a safe place to fall. Your dad is trying to give her that."

Mrs. Conner reached across the table and placed her hand over Carly's. "It's harder for you. You receive the fall-out of your mom's actions, but you can't do anything about your parent's relationship. You have to stand on the sidelines and observe their decisions, good or bad, but you have no say in it."

Carly's voice choked with emotion. "I'm supposed to stand by and know that my mom is with some other loser, while my dad is lying in a hospital bed, and I'm not allowed to do anything about it? She makes me so angry, and this latest thing is the worst. I feel like I need to confront her about it."

"I can't say whether you should do that or not. You'll have to figure that one out on your own. I don't blame you for being angry. If I were in your place, I would be angry, too."

"Do I go talk to her? Demand that she go see Dad?"

"I don't know, Carly." Mrs. Conner wiped a tear that had slid from her own eye. "I doubt it will do any good. This is between your parents. But if you feel you should, then maybe you should."

The compassion and love that shown through Mrs. Conner's eyes comforted the ache in Carly's heart. She felt herself relax again. The shaking stopped. She took a deep breath.

"If nothing else, it really helps me to talk with you about it. I still don't know what to do, but maybe I don't have to do anything. Maybe I need to wait."

"You could do that."

Carly looked around and stirred in her chair. "I have to get home. Uncle Walter was going to stay with Grandma for a while so I could visit Dad. I need to get back before he has to leave for work. Thanks for taking time to talk with me about this."

"Anytime, sweetie. I'm glad to listen."

"You are always a help, Mrs. Conner."

Carly's heart felt peaceful as she drove home. She didn't need to worry about this. None of it was her responsibility. She could be there for her dad and let him handle things with her mom however he wanted. It was her only option in this difficult situation.

Chapter Twenty-nine

Carly drove by her parent's house later in the week on her way to the hospital. Mom still hadn't been to the hospital to see Dad. Dad was improving every day. He didn't remember the accident, but he did remember working on a project in the garage

Carly hadn't been able to reach her mom on the phone. She decided she should stop by the house to make sure everything was ready for her dad's homecoming.

Mom's car wasn't in the drive, and the house was empty and quiet when Carly went inside. All the blood had been cleaned up. Carly looked in the refrigerator. It was almost empty.

Carly walked back to her parent's room. This time, her mom's drawers were empty. The piece of cardboard in the back of the bottom drawer had been removed. The pictures were gone. Her cell phone sat on the dresser, turned off.

A cold chill swept over Carly. Her mom was gone.

She felt like her mind was foggy as she walked to the front of the house, looking around for anything that might indicate where her mom had gone. An envelope sat on the end table by her dad's chair. Carly picked it up. She could see writing through the paper but didn't try to read it. She stuffed it in her bag and left the house, locking up as she went.

Will was working at the hospital this afternoon, and he'd promised to come by her dad's room, once Carly let him know she was there. Dad was sitting up in bed with his eyes closed listening to an audiobook. Carly knocked on the open door. He pushed himself up further and smiled at her, pausing the book.

"Hey! Good to see you!"

Carly forced a smile. "Good to see you, too, Dad. I see they are letting you entertain yourself."

Dad pointed at the iPod and speaker. "Only auditory stimuli," he said, trying to sound as if he was quoting the doctor. "No visual stimuli for another full week. After that, I have to take it on a day by day basis and see how I'm handling things. First sign of a headache and no more visual stimuli for me for that day. Oh, and lots of resting and naps."

Carly laughed, and this time it was genuine. "Oh, that is going to kill you!"

Dad gave her a wry grin. "I can't say I'm looking forward to it. I should be able to get a lot of 'reading' done as long as people will keep bringing me books to listen to. I'm not great at sitting."

"Grandma loves audiobooks. We check out a couple from the library every week. She listens to them when she's 'resting her eyes.' I have trouble keeping ahead of her."

"Do you have any recommendations?"

"Sure, if you like historical drama and romance novels," said Carly with a shrug.

"I can see your Grandma getting into those romance novels."

"You have no idea. She's worse than me!"

Dad winked at her. "You need some real romance in your life, not the kind you read about in books."

Carly blushed, thinking about Will. Then she remembered the reason for her delay. Leave it to Dad to lighten the mood. He'd always been the one to encourage her. She'd come to the hospital to cheer him up, but he'd still managed to make her feel better.

"Um yeah, about that…"

"Romance novels or you having a little romance in your life?"

"Romance in general, and romance in my life." Carly looked down, not meeting her dad's eyes.

"I can see you are trying to tell me something important. I promise not to interrupt again," Dad said, reaching up to pat the hand resting on his shoulder.

"You have to have noticed that Mom hasn't been here to see you," Carly said, bringing her eyes up to meet her father's.

His expression changed, his eyes filled with grief. "Yes, I had noticed. But I wasn't surprised."

"Dale and I spent hours trying to reach her. I got worried, so Grandma and I went over to your house to check if she was there and alright. I found Mom's cell phone. I called the lady from the art class, and she told me Mom hasn't been there in months." Carly paused, watching her Dad's face.

Her father radiated misery. He leaned his head back on the bed and closed his eyes.

"Mom came home while I was there and acted like you being here was no big deal. I encouraged her to come here to see you but she still hasn't, and I haven't been able to reach her on the phone since then." Carly stopped to collect herself, then took a deep breath and continued.

"I went by today on my way over here. Dad…She emptied all her things out of the closet. Her cell phone is on the dresser. We have no way of knowing where she is or if she is okay." Carly reached into her bag and pulled out the letter. "I found this next to your chair in the living room. I know I'm meddling by bringing it to you now, but I thought it would help. I can take it back there if you want."

Dad reached for the letter and looked at it. "I won't even be able to read it for another week unless you want to read it to me."

Carly pushed away the proffered letter. "Not particularly," she said with a grimace.

Dad took the letter and set it on the table beside his bed. Then he leaned back again with his eyes closed.

Carly walked around the bed and sat in the chair. She remained silent, waiting for her dad to speak.

"She'd already left me that morning." Dad's soft reply broke the silence.

Carly leaned forward. He kept his eyes closed. Carly waited.

"She told me she'd been seeing this man for several months. She told me this man would allow her to travel with him, see the world. He's rich…She wanted the things he was promising.

"I didn't beg her to stay. I told her I wished she would, that I loved her no matter what. She said she'd already stayed too long and that she deserved some happiness, too, the kind you didn't have to sneak around to enjoy. She told me this man was going to leave his marriage for her so she'd promised him she would do the same. She said she would be back for her things once she knew where she'd be staying." A tear slid down Dad's cheek as he spoke, but his voice didn't waver.

"I let her go. I couldn't stop her. I wanted to, but there was nothing that could be done. Her mind was made up. I decided to work in the garage on the deck furniture. That's all I remember." He looked over at Carly, an apology on his face. "I'm sorry you and Dale had to go through that. I'm sorry she rejected you both when she rejected me. It isn't fair to you."

"But it isn't fair to you, either." Carly could barely choke the words out.

"It isn't a surprise. I've suspected something was going on for a while. That's part of the reason why I told you about it.

"So much for romances, eh?" Dad finished with a mirthless laugh.

They both fell silent, each lost in their own thoughts. Carly sent a text to Will.

"About romances…I have someone I want you to meet. He works here at the hospital. He wants to meet you," Carly said.

"Is this that fellow that Dale was telling me about?"

"What did Dale tell you?"

"He said that you had a friend that came to the rescue when they brought me to the hospital. He said he works here and that he advocated for me when they brought me in."

"That's the one. Did he tell you anything else?"

"No. Why? Should I be concerned?"

Carly managed a laugh. "Well, probably. But you can decide for yourself. He's on his way here right now."

As if on cue, the door opened, and Will's face appeared around it. "Can I come in?" he asked.

Carly waved him in and got up to stand beside him. "Dad, this is Will. He's my…"

"Boyfriend," Dad finished. He sat and looked at the two of them for a minute, a funny look on his face. Then motioned for them to come closer. Carly returned to her seat. Will pulled a chair from another part of the room, walking over to Dad's bed to shake hands with him before taking his seat.

Dad sat looking at him for a little while longer. "How did you meet?"

"I'm the home care nurse that visits her Grandma," Will answered, meeting her dad's eyes. "We struck up a friendship, but I wanted to get to know her better. I asked her out to my sister's wedding. We've been having dinner together at least a couple of nights a week ever since."

Dad's eyebrows went up. "A couple of nights a week? That's pretty serious."

"I enjoy her company."

"How do you manage that around everything she does for her Grandma?"

"Most of the time, we eat dinner there at her grandma's house. That way she can be there, and we can still spend time together." Will seemed at ease as he answered her father's questions. Carly decided she was more nervous than him.

"Do you have your own place? What do you do for a living?"

"I live at home. I could move out, but I haven't yet because it helps my folks and it's nice to not come home to an empty house when I'm off work. Truthfully, I haven't been spending much time there lately." He glanced at Carly. "We've been seeing a lot of each other."

Carly blushed and smiled but kept her mouth shut. Dad's eyes never left Will.

"I work two jobs," Will continued. "I work for a home care nursing company five days a week and then work part-time here at the hospital filling in shifts where they need me."

Dad nodded and looked over at Carly for the first time since they'd begun their exchange. "He'll do." A grin spread across his face. "But you'd better promise to bring him around more so we can all get to know him."

"I think he and Dale already have a game night set up. You'll have to fight Dale for dibs," Carly said with a laugh.

"Well, I gotta get back to work. My break time is about over. But I've been looking forward to meeting you, sir." Will stood and offered his hand to her dad again.

Dad shook Will's hand firmly. "I look forward to seeing you again."

Will nodded. "See you tomorrow," he said to Carly.

Dad looked back at Carly after he'd gone. "Why were you keeping this a secret?"

Carly sighed. "I knew you were going to ask that. Dale did. I wasn't keeping it a secret. We were all busy with everything and I didn't think of it. He drove me to the hospital last Saturday, and that was the first chance I'd had to introduce him to anyone."

"What's going on tomorrow?"

"Company picnic. Can't say I'm looking forward to it all that much, but Will wanted me to go with him. It seemed like a good chance to spend time with him."

"Not looking forward to it because of him or another reason?"

"I don't get that excited about spending an afternoon with a bunch of people I've never met."

"Ah." Dad leaned his head back again. "Who is staying with your grandma?"

"Will's sister Alice is coming over. She and her husband live a couple of blocks over from Grandma. They have a little girl that Parker, her husband, adopted before they got married. Alice and Jasmine stayed with Grandma last Saturday while I was at the hospital with you. Jasmine and Grandma hit it off. Grandma is really looking forward to it."

"You've been busy since you moved out."

"What do you mean?"

"I don't remember you getting out with your friends this much before. Well, you used to, but not for a long time."

Carly sat back and thought about it. Dad was right. She'd gained so many new friends in the last couple of months. She'd stepped outside her comfort zone time and time again. She'd branched out and learned new hobbies.

"Who knew that the best thing that would ever happen to me was losing my job and having to move in with my grandma?"

Chapter Thirty

Saturday morning Carly got up early to meet the running club. Attendance was down this week following the race, but Carly didn't mind. She ran with the slow pace group and listened to a growing Olivia complain about how running hurt her back but that she didn't want to give it up. Carly couldn't help rolling her eyes behind Olivia's back and laughing. The woman liked to complain.

She hurried home and cleaned up, then fixed breakfast for Grandma and herself. Grandma was in a state. She'd brought out a box of buttons and beads and some thin ribbon as playthings for Jasmine. That, along with the stitching from the weekend before that Jasmine had said wasn't finished, should keep them occupied for a long time. If not, Grandma had found the box of watercolor paints and paper and some old card games like Go Fish and Old Maid. There were old comics from when Dale was little and a book of fairy tales they could read. Grandma had more planned than they could ever do in one afternoon.

Alice arrived before lunch, and the four of them ate together. Will drove up as soon as they had finished eating. He hugged his sister and Jasmine, then he and Carly were off.

Carly settled into the car and leaned her head against the headrest for a moment. She'd barely had a chance to sit all morning, and it felt good.

"I'm nervous about this," she said after a moment.

Will took her hand in his own. "You don't need to be. It's going to be fun."

"I'm not great at sitting around carrying on polite conversation with strangers."

"Who said anything about sitting around? It's sort of like a carnival with games. You are going to have a blast if I have anything to say about it. It's catered, and you don't have to talk to anyone but me all afternoon if you don't want to."

"A carnival?"

"Yep. They have a few rides but not that many. Mostly the kind that go round and round and make you sick. I can't ride them. But they also have games and prizes."

"I've never been to a carnival." Carly was grinning like a little kid. "I've always wanted to but never had the chance."

"It's going to be fun! Last year I took Alice. We managed to win enough tickets to get this huge brown bear that we took home for our mom. When she saw it, she laughed till she cried. I think she put it in the corner of her bedroom. Dad says he still wakes up and sees that thing and thinks an intruder is in the house watching him sleep."

Carly laughed, the anxious flutters in her stomach changing from nerves to excitement as they turned into the park hosting the picnic. She leaned forward to try to catch a glimpse of all the fun things ahead.

A gigantic red and white striped tent was set up in the center of a field. Smaller white tents had been set up around it. A swing ride and a carousel were already running, despite being only half full.

Will parked and looked over at Carly who was beaming with excitement.

"I had no idea you would be so eager for this. Ready to go have some fun?"

Carly clung to Will's arm as they walked to the carnival in an effort to hold herself back. Now and then she would point to things with a squeal.

At the entrance, Will received a handful of tokens for each of them. They could be used to play the games or ride the rides and even "purchase" food. He slipped his in his pocket and handed Carly hers. Then they made their way around the park and decided how they would use their tokens.

Carly enjoyed every minute of that afternoon. She didn't care if she won anything, but it turned out that Will was pretty good at some of the games and they accumulated a fair number of tickets. She forgot about the stress of the past week and threw herself into enjoying her time with Will.

As evening came on, they used some of their tokens to get food and found a place at one of the tables to eat. Will told stories about his younger siblings when they were growing up. Then they went out to the lake and took one of the paddle boats for a ride. When they reached the middle of the lake, Carly propped her feet up on the paddle housing and leaned back with her hands behind her head.

"My face hurts from smiling this much," she said. She rubbed her cheeks, forming her mouth into an "o" to try to stretch it out.

"I'm so glad you are enjoying yourself. I had a feeling you would. It's mostly for the folks with families, but girlfriends can have fun, too."

"Girlfriends. I like it when you say that. I've waited a long time to be someone's 'girlfriend.' I was starting to think it wouldn't happen."

"Same here," said Will. Both of them sat there soaking in the evening sunshine. "Your dad is pretty great. You look a lot like him. Come to think of it, you act a lot like him, too."

"You mean I grilled you with questions the first time we met?" Carly asked, not able to contain a giggle. "You handled it very well, by the way."

"I didn't mind. If I were a dad, I'd be the same way. I'd prepared for worse. Thought about bringing my W-2 and income tax returns, along with a criminal background check and credit report. But I decided that might be overkill." Will winked at Carly. She rolled her eyes and gave him a playful punch on the arm. Will faked a pout. He rubbed his arm until Carly pecked a kiss on the spot she'd punched. Then she slid her arm through his and leaned on his shoulder. They sat there together, floating in the quiet of the lake, the carnival sounds wafting to them over the water.

A few minutes passed before the man at the dock waved them in, and they started back. Will helped Carly out of the boat and onto the dock. Then they wandered back to the carnival to use up their remaining tokens. Will played his best games and won them tickets. When all their tokens were gone, Will gathered the tickets and handed them to Carly. They filled both hands.

"Let's see what we can get with these." Will said.

They found their way to the prize booth, just inside the carnival exit.

"You pick something," Will said when they started looking.

Carly looked around the little booth, unable to decide on anything. Finally, she turned back to Will. "You'll have to pick. I can't decide."

Without hesitation, he walked across to a medium-sized teddy bear dressed in scrubs. The man in the booth counted out the tickets they needed to pay for it. Then Will tucked it under his arm. Taking Carly by the hand, he led her out of the booth and toward the car. The sun was setting as Will unlocked the car and they got in. He looked at the bear in his lap for a moment. Then he handed it to Carly.

"This is for you. Every time you look at it, I want you to think about me and know that I'm thinking about you and that I care about you." Will met her eyes.

Carly forgot about the bear. She forgot about everything except the wonderful man sitting beside her. She reached up and kissed him on the mouth. The bear lay forgotten on the seat beside them as his hand came up to cradle her head and her arms went around his neck.

Will drew Carly closer and kissed her again. His lips moved over her cheek to a soft spot under her ear and then down to her throat. He drew back. His eyes caressed her face before coming to rest on her mouth. His lips met hers one more time.

With a sigh, he pulled away, his hand sliding down her arm until he was holding her hand. He leaned his head against the headrest on his seat and looked at Carly until she blushed. She'd picked up the bear and was holding it on her lap.

Will released Carly's hand and reached up to brush his fingers down her face. "Think of that every time you look at that bear."

Carly smiled at Will, touching his face in return. He caught her hand and kissed her palm before turning away, starting the engine, and backing out of the parking spot.

Carly groaned when she saw the clock in the car. "I had no idea how late it is! Alice and Jasmine needed to be home hours ago."

"Don't worry about it. I texted Parker that we'd be late and asked him to go over sometime in the afternoon. He said he was more than happy to do it, and then he could see that Alice and Jasmine get home safely."

"You thought of everything, didn't you," said Carly, reaching out to squeeze his arm again.

"I wanted you to have a day to enjoy yourself and not have to worry about anything."

"And I *have* enjoyed myself," said Carly. "More than I ever thought possible."

Chapter Thirty-one

The next day, Carly told Dale about Mom leaving. She expected him to get angry, to react in some way, but he didn't. His response was subdued, understated. At first, Carly thought it was because he was around his children. But then Dale lifted tired eyes to meet hers.

"I knew. I guess I've suspected for a while. That day that I told you about, when Jessie went over there, she told me she thought someone else was in the house with Mom, but she couldn't be sure. She said Mom wouldn't let any of them into the back of the house and got angry when the kids went into the toy room to play. Then, a few weeks ago on a Saturday morning, I had to have brunch with a client. He wanted to meet at this fancy place across town. When I got there, I thought I saw Mom sitting at a table with a man. I could have sworn it was her. But they left while we were waiting to be seated and I couldn't be sure."

Carly was relieved that she no longer was the only one carrying this secret. In some ways, it made dealing with everything easier.

Dale helped Dad home from the hospital the next day and made sure he had food in the house. Carly and Grandma went to visit him twice. Carly made meals her Dad could heat without having to cook.

"I can cook for myself, Carly," Dad insisted.

"Not this week you can't."

Dad shuffled back to his easy chair. "Now I know how people get bedsores. My body hurts from resting all the time."

The doctor cleared him to go back to work three weeks after his accident had occurred. Carly and Dale checked in with him several times that week to make sure he was getting home fine and wasn't too tired. He pretended to be annoyed that they were fussing over him, but Carly knew he was thankful they did.

One evening in September, Carly called her dad to see if he'd gotten home okay. He didn't answer right away, and when he did, his voice sounded shaky.

"Dad, are you okay? Do you need me to come over there? Are you feeling bad?"

"I'm fine. I'm not used to coming home to an empty house. That's all," he replied.

"Why don't you come over here for supper tonight? I made plenty. Will is coming later, and I know he'd be glad to see you."

The silence on the other end of the phone lengthened. Carly thought he was going to refuse.

"That would be a good idea. I don't think I should be alone this evening."

Carly sagged with relief and went to let Grandma know they'd have company for supper.

Dad stayed until after Will arrived that evening. The two men were soon engrossed in conversation and didn't notice that Grandma had gone to bed or that Carly was finishing the kitchen clean-up. Dad told Will about the deck furniture he was making, and Will got excited. He asked if he could come watch and learn.

Carly felt a twinge of jealousy as she listened to the men make plans.

"You know, most couples date one night a week, not every night," Nadine reminded her while they were running the next morning.

Carly sighed. "You're right, and I know it. I'm feeling a little selfish with his time."

"I don't blame you one bit, don't get me wrong. But your dad and your boyfriend need to get to know each other."

Carly knew it was true, but she still didn't feel like sharing Will with her dad.

That night Will called her when he got home from her dad's house. It was late, and she was already in bed. Her heart gave a happy little jump when she saw his name on the screen.

"I can't talk long," Will said, "but I missed being with you tonight. Wish I could be two places at the same time, or that you could come hang out with your dad, too."

Carly felt so much better. He'd been thinking about her. "Nah, he needs this time to get to know you. Did you guys have a good evening?"

"Yeah, we did." Will's enthusiasm radiated through the phone. "He showed me what he is making, and I was able to help. We talked a lot. He needs people to be around. I think he's feeling pretty low."

Carly's eyes slid shut. She'd been afraid of that. "Can't blame him there."

"No, you can't. If you don't mind sharing me, I'd like to spend some time with him. Get to know him."

"I don't mind. I did mind. Earlier today I was minding very much. But I fixed my attitude."

"Don't worry. I'll make time for us, too."

"Will, you are amazing."

"How's that?"

"I don't know how you do everything you do. You never stop, but you never seem to get tired."

"I get tired, but I feel like I've got to make up for lost time."

"Lost time?"

"I wish I'd have met you and your family years ago, but I didn't. Now I have to play catch up, get to know you and your family. And I'm enjoying myself. It hardly seems like I'm busy at all. Hey, I've got an early day tomorrow. But I'll see you tomorrow morning. Sleep well, Carly."

Carly smiled. "You, too. And thank you for everything."

Chapter Thirty-two

L ife settled into a predictable but welcome pattern. Dad came to eat dinner with them a couple of nights a week. Carly looked forward to him being there.

Summer turned into fall. The days stayed warm, but the nights were cool. Trees changed color. Will took Carly on a drive up the Great River Road to look at the vivid fall colors. They picnicked at a park along the way before heading home.

In the days following, Carly noticed that Grandma seemed tired, pale, not as eager to get up and do things. She spent almost all her time in her chair or in bed. When Carly tried to get her to help with the quilt projects they'd been working on, she'd participate for a little while, then doze off. She began asking for stronger pain medicine almost every day.

One morning Carly woke before dawn to Grandma coughing. She lay in bed for a few minutes trying to decide if Grandma needed help or not. When she heard Grandma gag and wretch, she jumped up and ran to her bedroom. She helped Grandma sit up in bed, and the coughing subsided. Then she got her a drink and helped her get settled in the living room so her head would be propped up. The cough hung on all day.

Will looked concerned the next morning when he visited. He listened to Grandma's chest, a worried frown on his face.

"Have you called her doctor yet?" he asked Carly. She was working on breakfast dishes in the kitchen.

"I was waiting until you came to check her."

"You need to call them. It might be nothing, but she sounds congested deep in her lungs. I thought I heard it late last week, but it wasn't this bad.

I should have known better and suggested you take her to the doctor sooner."

"You didn't know," Carly said. She dried her hands and reached for the phone.

Will went back to the living room to continue his check-up. Carly joined him a few minutes later.

"The doctor can't see her until Friday."

Will took a deep breath, hands resting on his hips, looking at the ceiling. "We only have a couple of options. The first one is for me to call. They might take me more seriously. She needs to get in to see the doctor today. The second is to go to the emergency room, but then you are looking at a long wait in uncomfortable surroundings. The doctor is the best option."

Carly nodded her agreement and handed the phone and the doctor's number to Will. "I'll do whatever I need to do. Just tell me what that is."

The conversation was animated and heated. Carly had never seen Will get upset before. He stepped outside so he would not upset her grandma.

When he came back, he found Carly in the kitchen. His face was flushed, and his eyes were still flashing. He leaned on the back of a kitchen chair and took several deep breaths. Then he reached for the medication chart.

"This med is supposed to control your Grandma's edema. It is usually prescribed for people with the beginnings of congestive heart failure," Will said. "Has she been taking the medicine in the prescribed dose?"

Carly nodded. "Yes. She hasn't missed a dose."

"Good. Have you noticed any shortness of breath or swelling in her feet and ankles?"

Carly frowned. "Yes. To both. She has been walking like she is supposed to, but she's been getting out of breath when she does. In fact, since Friday she's been getting out of breath when she walks up and down the hall. I've been trying to get her to leave her feet up more because her ankles were swelling."

"I wish you'd have said something last week." Will's anguished expression frightened Carly.

"She does that sometimes when the weather is going to change, but then it gets better. At least that's what she says causes it. I blamed it on the weather."

Will's concern grew. "How long has she been using that as an excuse?"

"The whole time I've been with her, but especially the last month." Carly's voice fell to near a whisper, and her stomach clenched into knots. "Have I failed in the one job I had to do? All I had to do was monitor my grandma's health."

"No, Carly, you haven't failed. You've taken her to all her appointments. You've given her all her medication. I've been checking her three times a week and today is the first day I've noticed this. This is something her doctor should have been watching more closely." Will took a deep breath and looked at the table. "When was the last time they did blood work for her?"

"I don't think they've done it since the middle of the summer."

"Do you have a copy of the results?"

"I think so." Carly turned to look in the folder she kept on top of the refrigerator in case of an emergency. She flipped through the papers and produced the copy she had of the most recent blood work results. She handed it to Will.

Will looked at it and then handed it back. "They are refusing to see her any sooner than Friday. I think if you wait that long, she will be too far gone to recover." He paused. His jaw clenched and unclenched a couple of times. He gripped the back of the chair until his knuckles turned white.

"Here is what you need to do," he said. "Take her to her doctor's office. It's right next to the hospital. The worst they can do is turn you away, and then you can go to the emergency room. Pack a bag for her. They'll probably admit her to the hospital even if her doctor sees her."

"It's that serious?"

"It isn't serious yet, but if we don't act now, it will be."

Carly closed her eyes and took a deep breath to collect herself. When she opened her eyes, Will was watching her. Carly wrapped her arms around him and leaned against his chest, drawing on his quiet strength.

"We're going to do everything we can for her. Even if I have to take time off my job and stay there with you, she will get the care she needs." Will's voice rumbled in his chest against Carly's ear.

Carly pulled away from Will. "Let's get this thing going, then."

Chapter Thirty-three

C arly sat in the waiting room at the doctor's office for over an hour. The nurse glared at her when she signed in on the list, muttering about the full appointment schedule. Grandma dozed in her wheelchair. Carly worried that her feet would start to swell soon, but she didn't know what to do about it.

Carly tried to play a game on her phone, but the television was so loud she couldn't concentrate. She picked a magazine off the table and thumbed through it. None of the articles caught her eye. She shifted in her chair and wished the doctor would see them.

Finally, the door to the back of the office opened, and the doctor came out. Carly jumped to her feet and stepped forward to catch his attention.

"Excuse me," she said. "You said to call you if we needed anything. We tried to do that, but your nurse is refusing to let us see you."

The doctor looked up from his cell phone, startled. "I had no idea you were even here! How long have you been waiting?"

"Over an hour. I called before that."

"Did you call the exchange?"

"Yes. They said that since her doctor was in the office, I was supposed to call him."

"I'm sorry," the doctor said, coming over to her grandma. "I had no idea. I have rounds at the hospital right now, but that can wait for a few more minutes. Let's get your grandma back to an examination room." He pushed Grandma in her wheelchair through the door, calling for the nurse to get one of the rooms ready. She glared at Carly and went to do what he asked.

The doctor listened to her breathing and her heart, pressed on her legs, and checked her pulse and blood pressure.

"How do you feel?" he asked after a few minutes of quiet work.

"Not good," Grandma finally admitted. Her breath came out in a shaky sigh. "And I seem to be feeling worse as the day goes on."

"When did you start feeling this way?"

"Sunday morning, but I didn't really start feeling terrible until around the time Carly brought me here. I wish I could lie down," Grandma confessed. She looked up at Carly and reached for her hand.

"Oh, Grandma, you should have said something sooner. I would have gotten you to the hospital yesterday."

"I thought it was the weather."

The doctor studied Grandma's chart. "We are going to have to admit her to the hospital. She needs to be on oxygen, and we will need to check the doses on her medications. I'll call ahead and have her pre-admission done by the time you get there. Go straight to the nurses' station on the second floor. I'll be around to see her when I'm doing my rounds."

Carly nodded. "Thank you so much."

She pushed Grandma out of the doctor's office. It took them a few minutes to figure out how to go from the doctor's building to the hospital. Carly chafed at every delay, asking everyone they passed for directions. They found their way to the nurses' station on the correct floor. A nurse was ready for them.

"Mrs. Terrell?"

When Grandma nodded, the nurse motioned to a room near the nurse's station. "We have a room ready for you. The doctor wants you in bed and on an IV and oxygen as quickly as possible. Come this way."

Carly watched over Grandma like a mother hen the whole time they poked, prodded, dressed, situated, and settled. After what felt like forever, they finished the testing the doctor had requested and settled her in bed with the IV and oxygen. She'd been given the proper medicine and, exhausted, had fallen asleep. Carly sat in the chair searching her face for signs of discomfort.

With a gasp, she remembered that she needed to call Uncle Walter. And her dad. And Dale. She sent a text message to Dale and Jessie and then called Uncle Walter and left a message on his voice mail. Dad picked up the phone after several rings.

"Hey," Carly said in a near whisper. "I won't keep you because I know you are at work, but Grandma is in the hospital."

"Oh, sweetie, what happened?"

"She started feeling bad over the weekend. Will thought I should take her to the doctor. I did and the doctor put her in the hospital. He's supposed to be by later to check her again."

"Keep me posted," Dad said. He was quiet for a moment. "It's times like this when I wish I could get in touch with your mom."

"It isn't your fault, Dad. Mom made her choice. Now she has to live with it."

While Grandma slept, Carly went back to the car to get their suitcase. She'd packed clothing for herself as well, just in case.

The doctor arrived to check Grandma while she was away from the room. She returned as he was finishing his exam. He motioned Carly to follow him out into the hallway.

"I'm concerned that her oxygen saturation hasn't come up in the last couple of hours. There should have been a small improvement, but she hasn't improved at all. We're going to increase how much oxygen she is getting and give her some medication that should help, but I can't make any promises."

Carly glanced back into the room at her grandma in the bed. "What happened?" she asked. "How did I miss this?"

"She's had congestive heart failure for years. That's a ticking time bomb. Even with medication, we can only control the fluid buildup for so long. Eventually, it gets worse, and there's nothing we can do. We are going to do everything we can to take care of your grandma," the doctor assured her.

"I understand," Carly said.

She slipped back into the room. Grandma was awake. She smiled through the oxygen mask at Carly. "Don't worry about me, dearie. I'm going to be fine. One way or other, I'll be fine."

Carly's throat tightened. "I'll be here with you, Grandma, the whole time you need me."

"I know. I'm thankful for you, for all the time we've had together the last several months. Now, my game show is going to come on in a few minutes. Do you mind finding it on the television?"

Carly laughed around the lump in her throat. "Can't break the routine, eh Grandma?"

"And why should I? "Raise the bed up a little. It's going to strain my neck if I keep lying like this."

Carly watched the game show with Grandma, but she really didn't pay attention to it. Her gaze stayed fixed on the woman in the bed, watching to see if there was any little change, anything she might need.

Grandma would get better and go home. Carly was determined. She couldn't lose her, too.

Chapter Thirty-four

The whole family came to visit Grandma over the course of that night. Dale and Jessie came about the same time as Dad arrived. No one stayed long. Uncle Walter came before visiting hours were over.

Once everyone was gone, Carly started settling in for the night. The chair in the corner folded into a bed. She found sheets in the closet, and after she pulled the bed out, stretched them over the cushions that doubled as a mattress. Someone knocked at the open door. Carly glanced around in time to see Will stick his head inside.

"Oh, hi!" Carly exclaimed, surprised to see him. "Visiting hours are over. How did you get in?"

Will held up his badge. "I work here, remember?"

"Are you working now?"

"No, but I will be working tomorrow afternoon. Have you eaten anything today?"

"No, she hasn't," Grandma answered for her.

"It hadn't occurred to me," Carly said.

"I brought you some food. Don't get excited. It's from the cafeteria."

"Thanks," Carly said, taking the salad Will handed her. She went over and sat on the edge of the chair-bed, while Will sat next to Grandma on the hospital bed.

"How are you feeling now?" he asked, covering her frail hand with his own large one.

"As well a can be expected, I guess." Grandma gave him a weak smile. "I seem to have gone from bad to worse."

"We'll take care of you," Will assured her.

"Promise me you'll take care of Carly," Grandma said, trapping his hand between both of hers.

"Grandma, you're going to be…" Carly began, but neither of them was listening.

"I promise." Will's eyes stayed fixed on Grandma's, silent communication passing between the two.

"She is such a special woman. She deserves to be treated well," Grandma continued.

"I agree," said Will.

"I'm glad God brought you into our lives the way He did and when He did. We needed you."

"I needed you, too. You all have been the best thing that ever happened to me."

Carly felt a tear slide down her cheek. It sounded like they were saying goodbye. Grandma couldn't say goodbye to Will. She was going to be fine. She would be here for a few days and then get better and go home, just like last time. Carly set the salad aside, unable to swallow around the lump in her throat.

Will wasn't finished talking yet. "I'm going to ask her to marry me, Grandma. Are you okay with that?"

Grandma looked over at Carly. "Nothing else would make me happier. She deserves a wonderful man like you."

He leaned over and kissed Grandma on the cheek. She moved the oxygen mask and gave him one, too. Then he hugged her. Pulling away from Grandma, he stood and walked over to Carly. He pulled her to her feet and into his arms. There, in front of Grandma, he kissed her with all his heart. Carly relaxed into the kiss, gripping the front of his scrubs in her hands to steady herself.

Will held Carly close. She slid both arms around his waist and leaned her head on his chest.

"I love you," he said loud enough for Grandma to hear.

"I love you, too." They were words that had been burning in her heart for weeks now, but she didn't want to say them before he was ready.

Will looked over at the chair bed and saw the teddy bear on it. "I see you brought my bear." He grinned down at her. "If you need me tonight, anytime, don't hesitate to call. I can come up here even if the rest of the family can't."

Carly nodded against his chest. He released her slowly, planting one more kiss on her lips as he did so. Carly didn't want him to go, but Grandma was exhausted, and Will could see that.

After Will left, Carly ate the salad and got ready for bed. She made the room as dark as she could and settled on a chair beside Grandma's bed, holding her hand until the old woman fell asleep. Then she slipped across the room and onto the chair bed, determined to watch over her all night. But the sleeplessness of the last several nights finally caught up with Carly, and she fell asleep despite her efforts to stay awake.

***

Sometime near morning, Carly awoke to alarms in the room going off and nurses scurrying in and out. She heard voices saying things like "don't resuscitate" and "living will." She pushed herself up to a sitting position and looked over at Grandma. One look and she knew what Will and the doctor had known since yesterday.

Grandma was gone.

A peaceful smile played on her lips. She looked as if she were enjoying a pleasant dream. The grey pallor of death made her no less beautiful than she had been in life. Tears streamed down Carly's cheeks, and she drew her knees up to her chest as though to protect herself from the pain.

Carly looked around the room, at the people hurrying here and there to do things that didn't seem to need doing anymore. Then she thought of Will. A glance at the clock told her he'd be up getting ready for his day. She picked up her cell phone and dialed his number. He picked up after the second ring.

"Carly, are you okay?"

"She's dead." Carly managed to croak.

"I'm so sorry," came Will's voice full of his own tears from the other end of the phone.

"You knew," Carly whispered.

"I didn't know but I suspected. I've seen it before, Carly." He was quiet for another moment. "There was nothing else you could have done. You did everything right. It was her time."

Carly sobbed into her knees. "I could have brought her here on Sunday."

"It wouldn't have done any good. She should have improved with the treatment they were giving her. It was her time. Listen, I'll be there in a few minutes. Hang on till I get there."

Carly nodded. "Okay," she managed.

The doctor on duty came and talked to Carly. Carly didn't register anything he said except that they needed something signed. She told him they would have to wait for Uncle Walter to arrive. They disconnected all the tubes and wires from Grandma's body and took off the oxygen mask. Carly couldn't wrench her gaze away from her grandma, unable to believe she was gone.

Will found her there. He didn't try to disturb her. Carly had no idea how long she sat next to Grandma crying. It felt like minutes, but it could have been hours. After a while, Will touched Carly's shoulder. She turned toward him.

"You need to collect your things. They're going to be taking your grandma away. It's normal, but we don't need to be here for it. Your Uncle Walter will be here in a few minutes to take care of everything else."

Carly nodded. She stood as if in a dream and moved around the room packing her bag. In a few minutes, she was ready to go. Will led her out of the hospital and into the cold, fall morning sunshine.

Carly lifted her face toward the sun that was beginning to peek above the horizon and closed her eyes, letting the rays warm her face. Will stood next to her, holding her hand.

"She's in heaven with Grandpa. She has no more pain, no more difficulty breathing. She's happy." A tear slid down her cheek. "I wish it didn't have to hurt this much."

"She loved you, Carly." Will put his arms around her and let her lean on him.

"She helped me learn how to be happy again. I'm going to miss her." She pulled away and looked up at the tall man beside her. "Thank you for helping me know it was time to say goodbye."

He brushed her tears away with his thumb. "I'm glad I could see her one more time, too."

Chapter Thirty-five

The morning after Grandma's funeral, Carly woke to a freezing house. The mild fall weather had given way to a cold front that came through during the night. Carly pulled the quilts up to her chin and curled into a ball in bed, shivering. Good thing Uncle Walter had checked the furnace last week.

After a few minutes, Carly reluctantly pushed the covers back. Grandma would be cold. She'd also need her pills and some breakfast. Carly swung her feet over the side of the bed and slid them into her warm slippers. Then she remembered.

Grandma didn't need her pills or breakfast anymore.

Carly shuddered all over, but this time it wasn't from the cold. She'd cried so much the last few days. Yet the tears came again as she pulled a hoodie over her pajamas and shuffled to the thermostat to turn on the heater.

She went to the kitchen and found coffee still in the pot from the previous morning. Carly poured herself a cup, then sat on a kitchen chair with her knees pulled up to her chest as much to help with the ache in her chest as to keep her warm while she waited for it to heat. When the microwave beeped, Carly ignored it.

What was she going to do? Grandma didn't need her anymore. She didn't have a job. She could move back with Dad. He probably needed her. But it wouldn't be the same.

The warmth from the heater began to seep into the air in the kitchen. Carly stood and retrieved her coffee from the microwave. Then she shuffled through the house to Grandma's room.

It looked the same as it had that morning a week ago when Grandma had been sick. The blankets on the bed were mussed because Carly hadn't had a chance to straighten them before they left for the hospital. Grandma's nightgown lay across the end of the bed, and her dirty laundry remained in the hamper. Carly didn't want to touch any of it. The room stood as a time capsule, a reminder of a woman Carly expected to hear calling to her at any moment.

Carly turned away from the door. She couldn't go there today. She moved down the hall to the sewing room.

Uncle Walter and Aunt Ellen's quilt lay finished on a shelf. Carly and Grandma had planned to give it to them for Christmas. Carly touched the pieces of the quilt she was currently working on. She hadn't made much progress. Grandma had found the pattern in a quilting magazine and bought all the fabric for it but had never started it. Carly had started it the week or two before Grandma died.

Carly set her coffee cup to the side on the end table beside Grandma's easy chair. Then she took up the rotary cutter and started cutting the next pieces she would need, following the directions in the magazine. She was soon lost in her work. Carly didn't notice her coffee had cooled or how many hours had passed.

When the last piece had been cut and put into the proper stack, Carly straightened from her work. Her back was killing her, and she had a mild headache that was growing worse by the minute. She looked at the clock on the wall. It was late afternoon.

Carly looked around, saw her half-drunk cup of coffee, and realized she hadn't eaten anything all day. Without Grandma here, she'd lost track of time.

Carly went back to the kitchen and heated her coffee again. Then she dug through the refrigerator looking for leftovers. She found a casserole she'd made last week, and some Chinese food Will had brought the last time he'd been here for a date. Once she'd warmed all the food, she went to the living room and turned on the TV.

Carly half listened to the evening news as she ate her food. The doings of politicians and athletes around the country had little bearing on her own pain. However, when a blurb came on about a local man named Mark

Tripton, Carly sat up to listen. The news anchor talked about the man being investigated for insider trading fraud by the SEC, but Carly barely heard him. The face of the man from Mom's picture dominated the screen. Then the report cut to a video of the same man leaving a courtroom. Carly thought she could see her mom in the background next to a person that could only be one of his lawyers. The blip was short. Carly didn't have enough time to be certain.

Mom. She'd been so wrapped up with her own selfish desires and needs that she'd missed the death of one of the people who'd loved her most. She'd never get another chance to say goodbye. Carly didn't think she even cared.

Carly watched until the local news came on again. This time she was ready. When the report came on, Carly paid close attention to the scenes in the background. This time she was confident it was her mother. She'd lost weight, and Carly could tell her hair had been dyed to make her look younger. She didn't look happy.

Carly picked up the phone from its base and called her dad to see if he'd seen the news report. The phone rang several times and then was picked up by the answering machine. Carly hung up without leaving a message and looked at the clock. She'd lost track of time again. Dad wouldn't be home from work for half an hour.

Carly slid to the floor, not hearing any of the rest of the news or weather. She hugged her knees to her chest, numb to everything except her pain and loss until she fell asleep curled up on the living room floor.

***

A pounding on the front door jerked Carly out of sleep. Will's voice came from the other side.

"Carly! Are you there? Please, answer the door. I'm worried about you."

Carly sat up and looked around, disoriented. A sitcom played on the TV. The house was dark except the lamp next to the couch.

Carly pushed herself to her feet and staggered to the front door, still groggy from sleep.

"Thank God!" Will said as soon as Carly opened the door. He stepped into the house and gathered her into his arms. "I've been trying to reach you for hours, but you weren't answering your phone. I couldn't even imagine what had happened to you."

Carly clung to Will. Calm and relief spread through her. Will was here with her. He'd take care of her.

After a moment she pushed away from him and looked around the living room. "I don't know why I didn't hear my phone. I don't know where it is." Her voice sounded rough and gravely from lack of use.

Will caught her chin and turned her to face himself. "Are you okay?"

"How could I be?"

Will pulled her against his chest again and Carly clung to him. He led her to the couch, moved the untouched plate of food from the seat, and sat, pulling Carly down next to him.

"Have you eaten anything today?"

Carly shook her head against him. "I'm not hungry."

"I know, but you need to try. At least drink something. Have you been drinking like you should?"

Carly shook her head again.

"Ah, Carly, I should have come over sooner, as soon as I called and you didn't answer. I brought some food. Alice sent squash soup. It's perfect for a cold day like today. You can even drink it out of a mug if you want." Will stood and retrieved a bag from where he'd dropped it next to the front door. Then he sat down next to Carly again. He opened the bag and removed a container of soup, a spoon, and a napkin.

The delicious smell of the soup wafted over to Carly, and her stomach growled loud enough for Will to hear it. He chuckled. "Not hungry?"

"I tried to eat earlier, but it didn't appeal to me. It's all leftovers. Maybe they aren't any good anymore." She nodded toward the plate that sat on the end table.

"That doesn't look good, but I don't know if that's because it's bad or because it's been sitting out for a while. Here, I'll get rid of it." Will took the plate and carried it into the kitchen. When he returned, he took out another container of soup and a spoon.

"What did you do today?" Will asked as they ate.

"I worked on the quilt Grandma and I started before…" Carly choked on the words. "Obviously I didn't shower or anything like that. I didn't even think of it." The blush deepened when Carly looked down at the thick sweatpants and hoodie she was wearing and remembered she'd never changed out of her pajamas.

"You look fine."

"Did you see the news today?" Carly was anxious to change the subject.

"No. Why?"

"The guy my mom left my dad for is in legal trouble."

Will set his container down. "You're sure?"

"Positive. He's being investigated by the SEC. I saw my mom in the video clip they showed." She looked up at the clock. "If we wait for a few minutes, we can watch the late news, and you can see for yourself."

"Does your dad know?"

Carly shrugged. "I tried to call him earlier and got his answering machine. He wouldn't have been home from work yet, anyway. I couldn't leave a message on his machine. Not with this kind of news."

Will looked down at the bite or two of soup left in his bowl. "That's crazy. Maybe this will be what she needs to shake her up and make her come back."

"I doubt it." Carly stirred her bowl of soup without seeing it. "Mom never got to say goodbye to Grandma. Not that she cares. They haven't gotten along well in years. But still, it was her mom. She'll regret it someday." Carly started to set the bowl aside.

"No. Eat all of it," Will said.

Carly glared at him, annoyed. "What if I can't?"

"You need it. You'll make yourself sick if you don't. I promised your grandma I'd take care of you."

Carly grumbled, but kept taking bites until she had finished the container of soup. Her irritation dissipated and she looked around the living room.

"I must have left my phone on vibrate after the funeral yesterday. It's still in my purse. I came in and collapsed last night and then…I didn't think about it."

Will took the empty container from her and pressed a bottle of water into her empty hand. "Drink it. All of it. I'm not leaving until it's gone."

A sob caught in Carly's throat and she curled up on the couch against Will. "I wish you didn't have to go."

He put his arms around her and held her while sobs wracked her body. Long minutes passed, then Carly grew quiet and still. Will smoothed her hair back from her face. She'd fallen asleep against him, the water bottle untouched beside her. As gently as he could, he lifted her and carried her to bed. Turning off the lights, he locked the house behind himself, using the key he'd borrowed from Nadine upon his arrival. He returned the key to a worried Nadine.

"Is she all right?"

"Yes," Will said with obvious relief. "But she shouldn't be left alone for too long."

"I'm supposed to run with her tomorrow morning. I'll go over and check on her and see if she still wants to go with me."

"Good. Alice said she'd visit after Jasmine gets off school. I'll get in touch with her dad, too. Between all of us, we should be able to help her through this."

Chapter Thirty-six

Carly woke the next morning before dawn with a splitting headache. She groaned as she rolled to her side. The bottle of water Will had given her the evening before sat on the bedside table along with a note. *Drink upon waking. Repeat frequently throughout the day to prevent dehydration.* A huge smiley face filled the bottom of the paper.

Carly didn't argue with the note. Her mouth and throat were dry and scratchy. She chugged the bottle of water and then went to the kitchen to find more. Then she dumped the rest of the coffee and started a fresh pot.

An insistent knock on the back door startled Carly. She gasped and ran her fingers through her bed head, then looked down at the sweatpants and shirt she'd been wearing for the past two days.

"It's me!" came Nadine's voice from the other side of the door.

Carly shuffled over, opened the back door a crack, and peeked out.

"Do you remember our run this morning?"

Carly looked down at herself again. "I'm not ready. Besides, I don't have running clothes for this weather."

"What you're wearing is fine. Get your shoes," Nadine insisted.

Carly opened the door so Nadine could step inside, then went back to her room to get her shoes and run a brush through her hair. She pulled out another long-sleeved shirt to wear under her hoodie and grabbed a stocking cap.

Nadine frowned when Carly returned to the kitchen. "Aren't you going to get hot in all that?"

Carly looked puzzled. "It's cold out there."

"You'll warm up." Nadine hesitated. Concern for her friend filled her face. "Never mind. Try the run in that, and if it's too much, you'll know for next time."

Carly felt like her legs were lead poles. Her lungs burned in the cold air. She listened to Nadine talk about things. Normal things. She didn't want people to talk about normal things now that Grandma was dead.

"A position opened up at work yesterday. A girl had a baby and then decided not to come back after her six-week maternity leave. Human Resources wants to get someone in the position as soon as possible. I told them I knew someone who would be perfect for the job," Nadine said as they finished their run and walked up the driveway to their houses. She turned to face Carly. "I know you don't feel like it yet, but you should come by today and apply. I think you'll be a shoo-in. You worked in accounting before, didn't you?"

Carly looked at Nadine as though she was looking through her. "Yes. I did."

Nadine reached out and squeezed Carly's shoulder. "I know you don't want to think about this yet, but you need to. You need to get into a new normal routine."

"I don't want to cope with it. I want to wallow in it." She walked several steps before she continued. "I'll be by later this morning to apply for the job."

Later that morning, showered and dressed in clothes she hadn't worn in months, Carly kept her promise. Her suit jacket and skirt hung loosely on her. The running must have toned her more than she'd realized.

She filled out the needed forms and scheduled an interview for the following Monday. The human resources person looked over her papers to make sure everything was in order before Carly left.

"I see you have a gap in your work history that begins six months ago? What is the reason for that?"

Carly looked down at her hands. "I lost my last job when my company downsized. Not long after that, my grandmother's health began to fail, and the family needed someone to look after her full time. That's what I've been doing for the last six months."

She nodded and made a note on Carly's work history. Then she looked up and smiled at Carly. "Thank you. We'll see you on Monday."

Carly kicked her heels off as soon as she walked in the door at Grandma's house. She changed into something more comfortable and then went to the kitchen to find lunch. She'd just finished when Alice knocked on the front door.

Jasmine bounced into the house, chattering about her day at school. She looked around the room, puzzled. "Where is your grandma?"

Carly didn't know what to tell Jasmine. She looked to Alice for direction.

"Jasmine, we talked about this," Alice said.

A sad look passed over Jasmine's face. "Alice said your grandma has gone to be with my gammy and Marcus." She wrapped her arms around Carly's legs, and Carly reached down and lifted her off the ground. Then Jasmine wrapped her arms around Carly's neck and kissed her on the forehead. "You go sit on the couch."

Carly obeyed, settling Jasmine on her lap.

"Here," the little girl said, pulling Carly's head to her small shoulder. "When my gammy died, Parker held me on his lap and let me cry on his shoulder. I'll have to sit on your lap because you're too big to fit on mine, but you can cry on my shoulder if you want."

Carly laughed. She couldn't help it. But the laughter turned to tears, and the next moment she was holding the child close and crying. Jasmine stroked her hair and shushed her. Gradually, her tears subsided. She sniffed one more time and met Jasmine's serious eyes. The little girl smoothed Carly's hair back from her face.

"There, that helped, didn't it?" she asked.

The last of the tears shimmered in Carly's eyes. Alice sat next to her and offered a box of tissue. Then she put her arms around Carly for a hug.

"Now," said Jasmine, pushing away and climbing to the floor. "Do you know where the coloring books are?"

The two women laughed at Jasmine's straightforward request. Carly, still sniffing and blowing her nose, stood and led Alice and Jasmine back to the sewing room. She pulled out the coloring supplies. Jasmine dropped to the floor to color. Alice wandered around the room, touching things here and there, a look of pleasure on her face.

"Will said you made the quilt he gave us for our wedding."

Carly flushed. "It was my first try at anything like that."

"Your first? I would never have guessed. I show that quilt to every person that comes to my house." She turned to the sewing table where the new project was spread out in orderly stacks. "I see you're working on another one."

"That's my third quilt," Carly said. She pulled Uncle Walter and Aunt Ellen's quilt off the shelf. "I finished this for my aunt and uncle not long ago. I started that one before Grandma died. I made most of my progress on it yesterday."

Alice made an exclamation of surprise. "Yesterday? You are amazing, girl! You have so much done already!"

Carly opened the magazine with the instructions and showed her the finished goal. Alice stroked the fabric.

"Will would love these colors," she said. "Don't show him or he'll try to claim this one, too."

Carly liked the idea of Will claiming the quilt. "I wasn't making it for anyone in particular. Grandma bought the fabric years ago, and I thought I'd try to finish some of the things she started."

"I've always wanted to learn how to sew," Alice said. "My mom can sew, but I wasn't interested when I was younger. Now that I'm an adult I don't have time to do it."

"I'd offer to teach you, but I think I might have a job. I have an interview in the hospital finance department next Monday. Nadine put in a good word for me."

Alice settled in Grandma's easy chair. Carly took the swivel chair at the sewing table. She absently noticed one of Grandma's coffee cups sitting on the end table that she hadn't noticed the day before. Her heart gave a little lurch, and she looked away.

"I don't know what to expect. I worked my last job for fifteen years straight out of college."

"I think you'll like it down there," Alice said, watching Jasmine color a picture of a puppy. "The ladies there are sweet. You couldn't ask for better co-workers."

The two women chatted for the next hour until Alice reminded Jasmine they needed to get home to fix supper for Parker. Alice ran her fingers over the new quilt fabric again as she was leaving the room. "Will would love this," she murmured as she left.

Carly knelt next to Jasmine. "Thanks for letting me cry on you. It helped me feel better."

Jasmine threw her arms around Carly's neck again. "I knew it would. It helped me, too!"

The house was too quiet after Alice and Jasmine had gone. Late afternoon sun streamed into the sewing room windows. She looked at the pieces she'd cut the day before, the beginning of an idea forming in her mind.

She'd make this quilt for Will. It would be one last gift from Grandma to him.

Chapter Thirty-seven

Carly forced herself to get up early on Saturday morning in time to meet the running club. She arrived home just as Uncle Walter and Aunt Ellen pulled into the driveway. She parked on the street so she wouldn't block them and followed them through the back door.

"I thought we'd sort through some of Mom's things," Uncle Walter explained.

"I have to confess I haven't done anything in her room since before we left for the hospital," Carly said. "Her room is still a mess."

"Don't worry about any of that, Carly," said Aunt Ellen. "We knew there were some piles of junk in the basement that she wanted to get rid of for years. We were going to start there today. We aren't ready to deal with the hard stuff yet."

"We'd like it if you'd live here for a while. The house will be more secure if people see someone coming and going. If you don't mind, that is," Uncle Walter said.

Carly looked from her aunt to her uncle, surprised. "Sure. I mean, I figured I'd need to move back in with Dad. I can stay here. I have a job interview on Monday."

"A job!" Aunt Ellen exclaimed and clapped her hands. "That's fantastic! And it came along as soon as you needed it. Isn't that wonderful, Walter?" Aunt Ellen gave a loud sniff and hurried from the room.

"Don't mind her. Reminders of Mom's passing are hard for her to deal with. She'll be fine." Uncle Walter pulled out a hanky and blew his nose. Then he turned to the basement door. "I'll head on down there. You tell Ellen where I've gone when she's ready."

Carly leaned against the stairwell. "Do you want help? I haven't cleaned up from running. I'd be glad to help you carry," she called to Uncle Walter's disappearing back.

"I'm glad for the help."

Carly had seen the pile of items every time she'd gone to the basement to do laundry. Boxes of canning jars sat stacked to the ceiling next to slat back chairs that used to be part of a dining set and boxes of old magazines and Reader's Digest condensed books. Carly and Uncle Walter loaded them into the back of his pick-up. Aunt Ellen gathered all the plastic cool-whip tubs and mayonnaise jars that Grandma had collected over the years and put them in the recycling bin.

Carly went upstairs to shower. Uncle Walter and Aunt Ellen were still sorting through Grandma's belongings when she finished. She ate some breakfast, then made her way into the sewing room to work on Will's quilt.

Uncle Walter found her there in the early afternoon. He poked his head in the door to let her know they were leaving.

"I spent hours in here with Mom when I was a kid," he said, a small smile playing around his mouth. He looked around, then stepped inside the door. "She'd help me with my homework while she sewed." He walked over to the sewing table. "I see you have another quilt started. This is lovely, Carly."

Carly fingered the pieces of the project she was ironing. "It's another one that Grandma wanted to make but never got the chance."

"Ellen doesn't sew, and neither does your mom. I think it's only fitting that these things pass to you. Mom would have wanted it."

Carly dropped into the sewing chair. "All of it?"

"Well, all of it that you want to keep." Uncle Walter looked around the room. "I loved her quilts. She made them with love and care. Each one was a masterpiece in its own way. Your grandma got to teach you how to do it. I'm glad to see you carrying it on. You enjoy all this. Well, Ellen and I are leaving. If you need anything, you let us know, you hear?"

Carly followed Uncle Walter to the back door, closing and locking it behind him. Then she searched through the fridge, looking for some lunch.

Her cell phone chimed with a text message as she put a plate of leftover pizza into the microwave.

Can I come over this afternoon?

Carly dropped the cell phone onto the table and turned away. Aside from a couple of short text messages asking her how she was doing, she hadn't heard from Will since he came over to bring her soup.

Hurt tears stung her eyes when she thought about all he'd said to Grandma about taking care of her. Another chime, another text message. Carly sighed and leaned her head against the cupboard as the microwave beeped. She reached for the phone.

I'm coming. See you in a few minutes.

Carly took the pizza from the microwave and sank down at the table to eat. She'd been making excuses for him for the last several days. He was busy. He worked two jobs and sometimes took extra shifts. He'd been spending time with her dad doing some building project.

But she missed him. He used to come over three days a week to check Grandma. Even if she couldn't see him any other time, she'd see him then. Then there were the late dinners, the movie nights, the times they'd run together on Saturday. Carly pulled her knees up to her chest and leaned her forehead on them. Grandma's death had changed so many things.

A knock sounded on the front door.

Carly went into the living room to open it.

Will stepped inside. Relief washed over his features when he saw Carly. "I've been worried! I've been trying to get in touch with you since yesterday." He reached out to her.

Carly pushed away. "What are you talking about? The text message you sent a little while ago is the first time I've heard from you in days."

Will caught Carly's shoulders. "I've been calling your Grandma's phone."

Carly pulled away from Will and stalked to the end table where the phone sat. The answering machine sound had been turned off as had the phone in the living room. The only other phone in the house was in Grandma's room, and Carly was certain the battery was dead.

The number on the answering machine indicated it contained twelve messages.

Carly turned back to Will. "I don't know who turned the sound off on this. I didn't hear it ring even once. I thought you'd been ignoring me."

"I turned it off the other night when I was here. I wanted you to be able to sleep without being disturbed. I figured you'd turn it back on when you got up. But I worked my regular jobs and did two extra shifts at the hospital since then."

"Why didn't you try my cell phone?"

"I don't know. I guess I thought you'd be home." Will leaned his forearm on the doorjamb and rested his head against it. "I'm not doing very well looking out for you, am I?"

Carly felt the irritation drain out of her as she looked at Will for the first time since he'd arrived. He had dark circles under his eyes and at least two days of growth on his chin. His scrubs were rumpled.

Carly laid her hand on his cheek. Will covered it with his own. Then he turned his face and kissed her hand.

"When was the last time you slept?" Carly asked.

Will pulled Carly back into his arms. "What day is it?"

Carly laughed. She wrapped her arms around him and leaned against his chest. "I've missed you."

Will rested his chin on her head. "I've missed you, too. We got used to coasting, knowing we'd see each other at least three times a week. Now we'll have to start being more intentional. We'll have to make plans. I might have to take you out on a real date."

Carly pulled away and looked up at him. She saw a twinkle in his eye in the absence of a smile on his lips.

"Oh, horrors," she gasped.

Will chuckled and leaned down to kiss her. "I'd take you out right now, but I think I might put both our lives in danger. I'm too tired."

"Are you safe to drive?" Carly asked.

"I think so. I'll sleep better in my own bed. But I'd like to take you out Monday night if I could. I have to work a shift at the hospital tomorrow and then my regular job on Monday."

"I'd love that."

"Good, I'll see you then." Will kissed her again and then turned to go. "I'll text you when I get home."

When Will was gone, Carly went back to his quilt. Her irritation with Will had dissipated. She no longer felt like she was putting in time to get a project done. Instead, the quilt felt like a labor of love, a gift that Grandma would have wanted to make for him. Carly was excited to finish it and give it to him.

Chapter Thirty-eight

"What are you planning for Thanksgiving?" Will asked over breakfast one day a week before the holiday.

Carly was finishing orientation at her new job at the hospital. She and Will had been taking advantage of his hospital shifts to see each other. The coffee shop up the road from the hospital had the most delicious breakfast options.

Carly sipped her coffee and thought about the question. She didn't know the plan for Thanksgiving. Mom, Jessie and, Aunt Ellen usually took care of that.

"I don't know. I guess I need to call Aunt Ellen or Jessie to see what they've decided."

"Do you think you'd be able to get together with my family for a little while next Thursday? You're welcome to bring your dad, so he doesn't get stuck home alone."

"I'll call around, ask about it, and let you know," Carly promised. "Dad's having a hard time right now. He depended on Mom to make things festive around the holidays."

"I noticed that," Will agreed. "I stopped by there the other night to work on our project, and he seemed really down."

Carly frowned. "Do you think the reports about Mom's boyfriend on TV are making it worse?"

"They couldn't be helping. I don't know your mom, but she looks unhappy and unhealthy to me. It's got to be killing your dad knowing there is nothing he can do."

"Can't or won't?" Carly couldn't keep the irritation out of her voice.

"What could he do, Carly? March in there and demand she come back? That could make it worse. Sometimes I wonder if she stays away just to prove a point to your dad—that she doesn't need him, no matter how bad it gets for her." Sadness filled Will's eyes as he looked at Carly. "When he talks about her, he's always gentle and loving. You'd never guess by hearing him that she's left him. It's like he's waiting for her to get back from a long trip."

***

Carly mulled over Will's words. The first weekend of December, the inquest showed that Mark Tripton was guilty of insider training. He would be sentenced the first week of January.

Carly went to see Mrs. Conner that Saturday. Carly hadn't seen her since her since Grandma's funeral.

They chatted for a minute or two. Then Carly came right to the point of her visit.

"I'm sorry that I come over to dump my problems on you, but I'm struggling with something. I'm sure you've seen the news about this Mark Tripton fellow on television. He's the guy my mom ran off with a few months ago."

"Oh, Carly! I'm sorry!" Mrs. Conner reached across the table to squeeze Carly's hand. "It must be torture to watch the news and see that."

Carly nodded and swallowed hard. "The worst is seeing how it's affecting my dad."

"You don't know what to do for him, do you?"

"No, I don't. Especially around the holidays. Mom was the one who made things festive. She decorated the house and baked goodies and…and it's like Dad doesn't know what to do with himself this year. I don't know how to help him."

"Well, aside from suggesting you help him with the decorating and baking, I'm not sure what to tell you." Mrs. Conner looked at Carly over her glasses. "Your dad has to make his own choices.

"How are you doing, Carly?" Compassion filled Mrs. Conner's eyes as she looked at the young woman across from her.

"I'm grieving my grandma, hurting for my dad, and angry at my mom for betraying our family. Other than that, I'm okay." Carly sighed. Then she gave the older woman a smile. "A few months ago, I would have been debilitated by everything that has happened. Now, even with all these difficulties, I still feel happy. God is giving me peace and strength even when I don't have much of either myself."

When Carly left the Conner's house, she knew what needed to be done. She drove to the grocery store, calling her dad along the way.

"Hey, Dad," she said when he answered. "How about I come over, and we bake some cookies together. Or make fudge. Or whatever you want to do?"

"Will is here. Do you mind if he bakes with us?"

"He needs to get familiar with the Warren family recipes," Carly said. "I'll be there in a few minutes with supplies."

***

"Hey, beautiful!" Will called from the front steps when Carly arrived at her parent's house. He met her at the car to help her unload the groceries.

They carried the supplies to the kitchen. Then Carly returned to the living room to turn on some Christmas music. As the mellow sounds of a saxophone playing "Let it Snow" filled the house, Carly returned to the kitchen. The men were arranging the baking goods on the counter in some sort of order that only made sense to them. Carly found her mom's Christmas apron and tied it on.

"It's alphabetical. Should make it easier to find what we need," Will said, indicating the items on the table.

Carly rolled her eyes. "Sure, whatever. As long as it makes sense to you. All right, guys, what do you want?" she asked, pulling the worn box with recipe cards off the top of the fridge.

***

Hours later, they talked and laughed over warm cookies and milk. Will and Dad took turns beating the fudge until it was creamy. Then they put frozen pizzas in the oven to bake and started cleaning the kitchen.

"You know what this house needs?" Will asked, taking a clean plate from Carly and drying it.

Carly and her dad exchanged a look. "No. What?"

"Christmas decorations. We should put up some decorations while we're at it."

Carly's dad stood from his seat at the kitchen table. "I agree. I'll go start pulling the boxes out of the garage. You can help when you finish."

As soon as he was gone, Will wrapped his arms around Carly's waist and kissed her below the ear.

"You are terrible," she said. "You were trying to kick him out so you could kiss me."

"Nah, I really want to help put up decorations. Mom did it without me at home. In her defense, I did work two extra shifts that week. I only went home to sleep and shower." He smoothed her hair back from her face and then leaned his cheek against Carly's.

"You know how they say the way to a man's heart is through his stomach? Well, I had no idea you were such a good cook."

"You guys helped a lot. Mom has good recipes." Carly stopped and listened for a minute. "Dad's coming." She tried to scoot away from Will in the tiny space between herself and the kitchen sink but couldn't quite manage it. She grabbed up a wad of soap bubbles and flicked them at him.

Will jumped back with a laugh and then popped Carly with his drying towel. Carly scooped up another heap of bubbles and was all set for the attack when Dad entered the room.

"All right you two. I thought the goal was to clean up the kitchen, not make it worse."

"She started it," said Will, popping the towel in Carly's direction again.

"I did not!"

Dad raised an eyebrow. "Me thinks you both protest too much." Then he continued to the living room with his box of decorations.

Will winked at Carly. He took the next dish from the drying rack and continued with his work.

"I did not start it, Mr. Flirt," Carly muttered so only Will would hear her.

"Keep it up, and I'll kiss you right in front of him. I'll lay a good one on you, too."

Carly glared at Will. His eyes held a challenge, daring her to give him a reason to kiss her. She blushed and turned back to the dishes.

When Carly finished scrubbing the cookie sheet she was working on, she rinsed it and turned to put it on the drying rack. Will stood, hand out, palm up, a small black box sitting on his hand. Carly looked from the box to Will and back again.

"It's for you," Will said, opening the box. "I have a romantic dinner planned for our date on Monday, but I think this is the perfect moment." He cleared his throat and dropped to his knee. "Will you marry me?"

"Yes. Of course!" A tear slid down Carly's cheek, but she laughed with joy as she said it.

Will stood and slid the ring on her finger, then kissed her. "I love you," he whispered as he wrapped his arms around her and pulled her close for another kiss.

"I love you, too," Carly said when she could talk again.

Her dad came through with more decorations. "I was starting to think you were never going to ask her! The suspense has been killing me!"

Will and Carly burst out laughing.

Chapter Thirty-nine

Christmas morning dawned clear and cold. The sun was rising as Carly stretched in bed and listened to the quiet house. She wished she could go back to sleep but realized it was useless to try. She thought back to her birthday, so many months ago, and how she'd wished she could sleep more that day as well. Today, peace filled her. She lay in bed relishing the quiet.

She looked around her bedroom. An offer had been placed on the house right before Thanksgiving. Uncle Walter had informed the family of it on Thanksgiving Day. Carly packed her things, little by little. Most of Grandma's belongings were sorted and divided among the family. A few remained. The new owner had purchased some of the furniture, the refrigerator, and the washer and dryer. Closing was set for the first week of January.

Carly rolled to her side and sat up, looking around the sparsely furnished room. She'd be moving back to Dad's this next week. Boxes full of her belongings and items from the sewing room were stacked against one wall. Her suitcase sat open on the floor at the end of the bed.

Carly walked across the hall to Grandma's room and sank cross-legged onto the floor. She closed her eyes and let her mind wander. The room still smelled like Grandma—face powder mixed with the floral scent of her favorite perfume. Since Thanksgiving, this had become her morning ritual, remembering, saying goodbye every day.

She longed for her mom to come. Carly let herself daydream about what it would be like if she showed up today at her dad's house, having had a change of heart that made her leave whatever empty life she was living and return to the family she'd abandoned.

She looked down at her left hand where the diamond ring from Will sparkled, all shiny and new. Carly wished her mom was here to help with wedding plans. Aunt Ellen and Jessie were helping, and Alice had offered to do whatever Carly needed her to do, but it wasn't the same as having her mom there to help.

Carly knew her mom wasn't happy. She thought back to all the happy Christmases they'd had. Mom loved Christmas.

Carly pushed herself up off the floor. She had to get over to Dad's to help. Dad had put forth a valiant effort this year once Will and Carly helped him decorate the house. He was preparing brunch at their house with the family, just as Mom did every year.

When she arrived at her dad's a couple of hours later, the smell of ham and sausage met her at the door. She followed her nose to the kitchen where Dad stood slicing the ham with an electric knife.

"Grab an apron," Dad said, pointing with his elbow to where they hung next to the fridge. Dad stopped for a second. "You look nice. Very Christmas-y."

"Thanks. You look nice, too. And the house smells good! I'm hungry!" Carly grabbed an apron and tied it on. Then she took over stirring the sausage on the stove that would eventually be made into gravy.

Jessie and Dale breezed in, bringing with them the smell of warm donuts and biscuits. Jessie came into the kitchen and put the items in the oven to keep them warm, then helped Carly with the scrambled eggs. By the time Uncle Walter, Aunt Ellen, and Will arrived, the food was ready and on the table.

The family gift exchange took place in a flurry of activity. Carly and Will stood back in the archway between the living room and dining room watching the children open gifts first. With a giggle, Dale's oldest daughter, Lexi pointed above their head to the mistletoe.

"Look! Will and Carly need to kiss!"

The room grew silent as the family turned to look at them. Will looked down at Carly, his eyes warm. He slid his arm around her waist and pulled her against him. Carly leaned into his kiss, gripping his sweater in her fists. They finished to claps from the adults and squeals and cheers from the children.

Carly reached for the large package she'd set off to the side of the other gifts and handed it to Will.

"This is from Grandma and me."

He tore aside the wrapping paper, gripped the fabric backing, and pulled the quilt free. It unfolded, revealing the intricate quilt pattern.

Will's grip softened. Gently, he lifted the rest of the quilt free. "Carly, it's beautiful. Did you make it?" he asked, his voice soft and filled with awe.

Carly flushed. "Yes. Alice told me you'd like the colors. I decided to make it for you from Grandma and me. She would have wanted you to have it. It's how she showed people she loved them. I know she loved you. I love you. Every time you wrap in it, you can imagine our love wrapping around you."

"That's beautiful." Will's hand came up and caressed her face. He leaned and brushed his lips across hers. "I can hardly wait to use it."

He folded the quilt and tucked it back in the wrapping paper. Then he took Carly's hand and pulled her toward the kitchen. "Come on," he said. "I want to show you something."

Carly followed Will out of the kitchen door onto the deck. The deck chairs Dad made last summer sat on the deck. Next to them sat a brand-new set of chairs, complete with end tables and a picnic table. A red bow was positioned in the center of the picnic table, and a white envelope stuck underneath it. Carly stepped forward, picked up the envelope, and opened it.

Merry Christmas. Patio furniture for your patio. May you enjoy many days basking in the sun in your backyard. All my love, Will.

Carly looked around at the furniture, beaming. "It's beautiful! Now we need a patio to put it on."

He held a paper out toward her. Carly took it from him, confused.

"It's the title to a house. Our house."

"We don't have a house."

Then she recognized the address on the title.

"You bought Grandma's house?"

"I love the house. It has character. It holds a lot of memories for you, too. Alice and Parker like living in the neighborhood. It seemed like a smart move. Besides, I didn't figure you'd want to live with my parents after we got married."

Carly threw her arms around Will's neck. "Thank you! This is almost too good to be true!"

Later that night, Carly floated home to Grandma's house. No Will's house...Her house. She touched the walls and the furniture that he had bought. She looked at the boxes stacked in the bedroom, knowing she could unpack most of them, at least for now. They could decide how to rearrange things later.

This was her home now and would be for a long time. She knew Grandma would be happy.

Chapter Forty

Carly woke up the morning of her birthday and stretched, bumping Will's foot with her own. He muttered something in his sleep, and half rolled over without waking. Carly turned to look at him and smiled. She would have dropped off again if she didn't need to go to work. Will had worked a late shift at the hospital. He couldn't have been home for long, but Carly hadn't heard him come in.

She pushed herself out of bed and slipped out of the bedroom to the kitchen. A large bouquet of pink roses greeted her, along with a hot cup of coffee and a breakfast sandwich from the coffee shop near the hospital. Carly grinned and picked up the note propped on the flowers.

"Happy birthday, sweetheart! Love you! Hope you have a wonderful day and prepare to be pampered tonight after work."

The sandwich was still warm, and the coffee was the perfect temperature to drink. Carly ate, then dressed and left for work. When she arrived at the office, she found her coworkers had left balloons and a coffee mug on her desk.

Nadine greeted her with a hug. "Happy birthday! We'll have cupcakes after lunch from that little gourmet shop up the road!"

Carly appreciated her enthusiasm. "Any excuse, eh? Good thing there are only five of us in this office, or we'd have to do more than jogging to keep our girlish figures."

"Girl, I run so I can enjoy these things guilt free." Nadine patted her trim waist.

Carly's coworkers had accepted her into their midst and made her part of the group. She'd never felt this way about people from her last job. All the ladies had attended her small wedding in the spring. They'd given her a bridal shower, and they'd come to the open house when she and Will moved into Grandma's house.

The morning passed quickly. They savored the cupcakes at lunch and then Carly settled into the afternoon paperwork. The workday was almost done when her cell phone rang.

Carly glanced at the number on the screen. It was listed as "unknown." She didn't take personal calls during work hours. She pressed "ignore." A minute later, the phone rang again. Again she ignored it.

When the phone rang the third time, she called to Nadine, "I think I'd better answer my phone in case it's an emergency."

Nadine was on the phone but gave Carly a thumbs up.

"Miss Warren?" the voice on the other end asked.

Carly started to correct the person on the other end but stopped herself. "Yes? How can I help you?"

"Your mother, Susan Warren, was admitted to the hospital this afternoon. She's listed you as her next of kin."

Carly sat in stunned silence. Why had she given Carly as the next of kin? Why not Uncle Walter or even Dale? And why on earth was her mother in the hospital?

"Miss Warren?"

"I'm...I'm confused. I haven't had any contact with my mom in almost a year. I would have thought she'd have contacted my dad."

"She listed you as her next of kin," the person repeated as if that explained everything. "She is in ICU in serious condition. We need you to come to the hospital and review her treatment options."

"I'll be there as soon as I can arrange things here at work. Thank you for calling." Carly hung up her phone and laid it on the desk. She stared at the computer screen in front of her without seeing it until Nadine approached her desk.

"You have any celebration plans this evening?"

Carly didn't answer right away. "My mom is in ICU. They just called to tell me."

Nadine knelt by Carly. "Carly, I'm sorry. Do you need to go?"

Carly stood. "I think I should. I'm not quite done with this form, but I can finish it first thing tomorrow."

Nadine looked at the paperwork on the desk and then at the computer screen. "I'll take a minute and finish this one. You get up there and find out what is going on with your mom."

Carly gathered her things and set out for the other side of the hospital. When she reached Intensive Care, the floor nurse showed her to her mom's room.

She stopped outside the closed door and made no move to open it. "I have to warn you. Your mom is in very bad shape. She probably won't look like you remember her. We have her sedated and on a ventilator because she was unable to breathe on her own. She's had an extreme head trauma and she won't remember things from visit to visit."

Carly stepped up to the window and stared into the darkened room. A horrible sight met her eyes. The nurse's warning had not prepared Carly for the extent of her mom's injuries. Her face was covered with bruises, some a fresh black, red, and blue, others green and yellow. Blood had pooled and dried in her hair and in some places her hair had been completely yanked out. Her face was so swollen that Carly wouldn't have known it was her mom unless the nurse had told her. Bruises covered her arms.

Carly covered her mouth with her shaking hands. "What happened to her?"

"We don't know. EMTs picked her up at a hotel late this morning. She couldn't talk, but she gave them her cell phone with your number punched in. When they asked for her next of kin, she pointed to that. The police are investigating. You can get her personal effects from them."

"Can I go in and see her?"

"You can't stay long. She's heavily sedated. She won't even know you're here. The doctor will want to see you."

Carly slipped into the room and sat next to the bed. She looked at the woman in the bed and felt like she didn't know her anymore. This woman wasn't the same woman she'd grown up referring to as "mom." She hadn't been there for anything in the past year—Grandma's death, Christmas, Carly's wedding. Yet Carly felt no anger toward her, only pity. She thought of all the times in the past year when she wanted to tell her mom exactly what she'd done to hurt her, to make her feel like she had no value to the world at all. But when Carly looked at her now, she saw a woman who had been hurt far worse than she'd hurt others.

Carly felt a tear slide down her cheek, then another. She leaned her head over the bed and sobbed, begging God to spare her mom's life.

"Miss Warren?" The doctor's voice behind her startled her back to her surroundings.

"I'm...I'm not Carly Warren anymore. I got married earlier this year. But my mom wouldn't have known that. Now I'm Carly Stanton."

"I understand. Mrs. Stanton, your mother is in grave condition. It will take a miracle for her to live through the night. Judging by the extent of her injuries, she'd been abused for a long time, maybe even months, with the most extreme injuries occurring within the last six weeks or so. She has a brain bleed. We need to operate, but the damage to her windpipe and chest have left her in such a weak position that putting her under anesthesia could kill her."

"Was she with anyone? Who called the ambulance?"

"A hotel employee called 911. They said she was alone in the room when they found her. If you need any more information, you'll need to get it from the police."

Carly stayed a few more minutes before she left. She wasn't the one who needed to be here with her mom. She waited until she left the hospital for the parking garage before making the call.

"Dad, something's happened to Mom..."

Epilogue

"Visiting hours will be over in five minutes," the nurse said as she slipped the clipboard with Susan's medical records into the holder by the door and left.

Richard looked at his sleeping wife. He held her hand in his own, careful not to touch anyplace that was bruised or bandaged. He didn't want to contribute to her pain. His eyes traced every injury that he could see— the swollen eyes, cracked lip, split cheek, the large lump on her head that showed through her blood-matted hair. He saw the bone in her arm that rested at an odd angle and wondered if it was an old wound that hadn't been treated, or if the doctor needed to set her arm and they were waiting for her to stabilize first.

Then there were the internal injuries. The brain bleed and broken ribs. The bruising on her kidneys that had shown up on the MRI. Richard's heart constricted in agony for his wife's pain. What kind of a monster would treat another human being like this?

Susan's eyes began to twitch behind her lids. She groaned around the breathing tube in her throat, and her head thrashed back and forth. Her fingers twitched where Richard touched them, and he yanked his hand back, fearful that he'd hurt her. Her feet and legs jerked.

Richard dove for the call button and pressed it at the same time as a monitor in the room began blaring an alarm. The nurse flew through the door, followed by a doctor and two more nurses.

"She's seizing," the nurse said. "Mr. Warren, I'm afraid you need to leave now so we can work."

Richard stumbled back from the bed and out the door. He stood in the hall and watched them through the window as they labored over his wife's broken body.

"Oh, God, please save her. I love her so much. You love her so much. Let me have another chance to show her." Richard choked on the words, speaking aloud without realizing he had.

An aide touched his shoulder, and Richard nearly jumped out of his skin. He swiped at the tears on his cheeks.

"You need to go home. Visiting hours are over."

"I can't leave her like this," Richard said, his voice hoarse from the tears. "I have to know if she's okay when I leave."

"Okay. Go to the waiting room. I'll let you know as soon as she's stable."

Richard hastily retreated before the aide changed his mind.

Richard paced the waiting room floor. He stared blank-eyed at the news report blaring from the one TV in the room. (Maybe it wasn't blaring, but the noise made it impossible to hear if footsteps approached in the hall.) He finally turned the TV off and picked a magazine out of the rack. After reading the same sentence of an article three times without comprehension, he gave up and closed the magazine.

Endless minutes passed before the aide entered the room. Richard searched the man's face for any indication of the news he brought.

"She's okay—for now."

Richard dropped into the nearest chair. He sucked in a huge breath. Had he been holding his breath for the last hour? He felt like it. Now he gasped for air as relief flooded him.

"You'll have to wait until tomorrow to see her again," the aid continued. "I recommend you go home and try to clean up. Get something to eat. Try to sleep. The hospital will call you if there is any change."

"I could sleep here in the waiting room," Richard said. "Then I'd be here if anything happened."

Compassion filled the aide's eyes. "Mr. Warren, there is absolutely nothing you can do for your wife at this point. Exhausting yourself during the wait will only make it harder on you and won't help her."

Richard raked a hand over his face. It scraped on the stubble on his chin and cheeks. "I won't be able to sleep at home."

"I understand that. But you'll be able to take care of yourself, so you can take care of your wife when she comes around."

That wasn't what Richard wanted to hear, but he nodded in understanding and moved toward the door.

The aide rested his hand on Richard's shoulder as he went past. "We're doing everything we can for her. I promise we'll take good care of her."

Richard closed his eyes. When he opened them, he met the other man's gaze. "Maybe you'll take better care of her than I was able to." He rushed from the room and out to the parking garage.

He made it inside the car and slammed the door shut before all the emotions of the day exploded from him. Anger, fear, hopelessness, helplessness. He roared into the silence of the enclosed space. He pounded the steering wheel. Hot, angry tears streaked down his face.

The unexpected blare of the horn when he hit the steering wheel again brought Richard to his senses. He was breathing hard. He took several calming breaths and closed his eyes.

Peace filled him more and more with each breath. With the peace came hope. She'd be okay. She had to be okay.

Richard pulled his wallet from his back pocket and took out a picture he'd carried with him for years. He and Susan were seniors in high school. They'd been dating for most of the school year. The picture had been taken a couple of weeks before graduation. Susan's arms were around his neck, and Richard's arms were around her waist. She rested her head on his shoulder. He rested his on her hair. Her soft, silky hair. They were in love. Richard touched the picture and then bowed his head.

"Father God, you gave her to me once, long ago. Your gift to me. Will you give her to me again? I trust you to take care of her."

Richard leaned his head back on the headrest. Their future was uncertain. He didn't know how long it would take Susan to recover or if she ever would. Richard longed for a new beginning between them, and for her to love him as much as he loved her. But only time would tell if that dream would ever become a reality.

Lincoln Square Series

Talents, Book 1

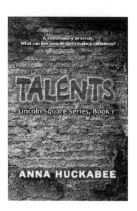

Parker Wilson has nothing more to worry about than his marketing job and donating bone marrow to his nephew who is fighting leukemia. Then he meets Marcus, a little boy dying of a brain tumor who spends most days alone in a hospital room. Because of this child's life and then death, Parker is forced to step outside his suburban comfort zone and confront the struggles, not only of one family, but of an entire community.

Available in ebook, paperback, and audiobook formats.

61098767R00107

Made in the USA
Columbia, SC
21 June 2019